The Green Palmers

Jon Huer

PublishAmerica
Baltimore

© 2006 by Jon Huer.
All rights reserved. No part of this book may be reproduced, stored in a retrieval system or transmitted in any form or by any means without the prior written permission of the publishers, except by a reviewer who may quote brief passages in a review to be printed in a newspaper, magazine or journal.

First printing

At the specific preference of the author, PublishAmerica allowed this work to remain exactly as the author intended, verbatim, without editorial input.
All characters appearing in this work are fictitious. Any resemblance to real persons, living or dead, is purely coincidental.

Illustrated by Min K. Seo

ISBN: 1-4241-3883-3
PUBLISHED BY PUBLISHAMERICA, LLLP
www.publishamerica.com
Baltimore

Printed in the United States of America

Written for Jonathan Blake Huer
for His 10th Birthday,
From Dad, with Love
May You Be Safe From Those Green Palmers
and to Terry Huer

Chapter One

As a testimony to the strange tale of evil that had almost lured the town's soul to sleep, the statue used to be much easier to notice. Time and repetition, along with other forces of nature, have made it less noticeable now. And thank Heavens for that.

Observant visitors to Laurinville, as they drove into town on the main highway, had no trouble spotting the life-size bronze statue of a boy. The boy has his eyes raised to the sky in earnest anxiety and resolve. Clutched in his hands with great determination is a picture frame the size of a small painting. Instead of a painting, however, the frame contains only an inscription, which says, "LIBERTY AND JUSTICE FOR ALL." Incidentally, the inscription has become the town motto of Laurinville since the Event.

The statue can be seen today only by those who are looking for it with more than casual interest. The robust presence of perennial flowers and unruly bushes, once planted around the statue only to highlight it, has simply outgrown and obscured its original purpose. Honeysuckles alone have grown so vigorously that they now cover much of the view of the statue. Like an important visitor whose every need is well attended to at first but whose subsequent familiarity soon breeds comfortable routines, the statue is now in a state of loving indifference.

I have been the one who has tried to keep it that way, somewhat against the wishes of some townspeople who want to keep their young hero more visible to visitors. But so far my sense of modesty has prevailed upon their civic eagerness every time the issue of renovation comes up. Why do I have such an influence on the town? Just by the sheer unfolding of fate, I must confess, with which my own will had so little to do. Life seems to be a large revolving stage on which will and fate take turns to tell their story.

Those with a keener observation might find that the face of the statue rather resembles one Michael Brown, a twelve-year old schoolboy at the time they erected it.

The caption on the plaque below the statue reads:

Dedicated to Michael Brown
A Boy Whose Bravery and Intelligence
Saved His Town from the Green Palmers.

That is quite a mouthful for a young boy. Even among most adults nowadays much of the dread associated with the memory of the Green Palmers has faded. The incident was almost like a bizarre nightmare which, once we wake up from it and realize what an utterly silly dream it was, we consciously try to forget. But there were times when the statue was more visible than today and the townspeople's dreadful memory much sharper than it is now. All the visible signs of the Event, which once dominated Laurinville's body and soul have now been erased from view. Aside from what is deeply lodged in their sometimes puzzling dreams, they might insist that the whole thing had come and gone like a summer shower—much sound and fury, but no lasting marks.

Now and then, some old timers still insist on reviving the

tale of good and evil, to which they feel they own the retelling rights. My insistence that the now-fading memories of the Green Palmers were actually much more sinister than retold, or that the heroic deeds of Michael Brown were actually much less heroic than recalled, merely falls on deaf ears. Naturally both good and evil are embellished in any retelling. So is the truth. I am quite certain about saying this simply because I *am* that Michael Brown, "Mikey" to my father and friends. I know what I did and didn't do.

Recently I have been repeatedly asked by Miss Miriam Raynor, our town historian of impeccable credentials, to tell the whole story from the viewpoint of my own involvement. She is compiling a ten-year review of the Event for the town annals and is of the opinion that my own account would be particularly valuable for her purpose. After all, Miss Raynor insisted, I was in the thick of it from beginning to end and (to quote her) "single-handedly defeated the invaders." A decade, she believes, is long enough for me to overcome my own reluctance to relive the memory.

Upon her irresistible and repeated urgings, I finally gave in and decided to tell the whole singular story from my personal experience.

I was seven years old when the tornado named Martha (one of the first tornadoes to be named) swept through Laurinville and killed 12 people. The only thing that I remember about the tornado itself was the vague sense of terror and excitement as we crouched on the floor at school, hearing the passing of Martha in a loud rumble as if a train was passing directly over us. It broke all the windows at our school. But it also broke my heart, for my mother was one of the victims. She was inside the house when Martha hit and caused part of the house to collapse on her. The town mourned its dead as if a heavenly edict had demanded its great sacrifice for no earthly reason. The town of Laurinville still bears the scar. One of the barns just outside the town stands half destroyed, now covered with wild vegetation and, although somewhat eroded by time, mostly unchanged.

My father worked, as he still does, as a baker at the town's only sweet shop. He has always been good at making specially-decorated cakes for birthdays, weddings, graduations, and anniversaries of all kinds. Often the caricatured decorations on the cakes are so humorous that the picture gets more attention than the person whose day is celebrated. However, his and the bakery's specialty was, as it still is, its fine array of doughnuts. Even today many townspeople make a special pilgrimage to visit the bakery and taste the doughnuts as they are served hot off the pan. Sometimes my father himself would come out from the kitchen to join them and take pleasure in their compliments on his workmanship. The customers would sit around at the shop's few tables, mostly laughing about non-events, sometimes exchanging views about the current crops and speculating on the upcoming weather.

As I was growing up this scene at the bakery always occupied my mind as if it were the essence of Laurinville. Our small-town life was without deep guile as it was without momentous events. Even with the tragic interlude of Martha, the town was really all laughter and small exchanges as I remember it.

Father always brought a doughnut or two when he came home late at night as a special treat for me. Of course, I had already gone to bed by then, often tucked in by my neighbor and babysitter Jamie Yarborough. She was good at making up a new bedtime story practically every night. At the time the Green Palmers came to our town I was already twelve and

Jamie, who was only six years older than her charge, had become my best buddy. Sometimes she still tried to treat me like the seven-year old grief-stricken child that I once was and I had to remind her how tough I had grown. She was still stronger and bigger than me, though, so I let her get her way most of the time. Besides, I was extremely fond of her.

On Sundays and Mondays my father was off work. On those days we would go to the town cemetery to visit Mother, sweep away the fallen leaves from the stone that marked her grave, and put fresh flowers in the vase. We almost never varied this routine. The only time we did not carry on with this routine was when I was sick with chicken pox. Sitting by Mother's grave, Father and I would tell her what had happened at his bakery and my school and some noteworthy events in Laurinville. When I had good grades to report I was especially delighted to tell her about them. Sometimes Father and I would have sandwiches there and even set a plate for her as if she were still with us.

Father was only in his early thirties when my mother died. He was a hardworking man known for his patience and honesty, and he was handsome. Naturally many widows and single women in Laurinville thought of him as a good man to get to know. Still very much in love with my mother, he was merely cheerful with their often obvious intentions and treated them courteously and respectfully. With one exception.

My father was particularly courteous and respectful with one Miss Terry Casey who was the only female auto-mechanic at a local repair shop. Her technical competence was well known. I often heard people whisper that she could fix problems that her male colleagues had given up as impossible. But she was so sweet and modest about her technical superiority that the male technicians felt no shame in asking her for help whenever they needed it. Even in a friendly town of infinite goodwill, and considering her business was known for its largely masculine nature, this tactfulness seemed no small accomplishment. Sometimes I watched her work under a car, grease on her mechanic's overall and even on her pretty face. She always took delight in teaching me about cars, showing me how each part worked to make the whole car run.

Miss Casey's husband, a fellow mechanic, was also one of the tornado victims. Whenever the town gathered to mourn its victims on anniversaries, I felt we should be as close as a family. Once my father's car broke down at home and Miss Casey came to fix it. While Father was describing the trouble to her they accidentally brushed each other's hands and both of them got red in the face and fumbled with words. When they noticed that I was watching the whole thing, they even got redder in the face and fumbled even more. I always thought they would make a nice couple. But apparently neither my father nor Miss Casey (everyone in town called her Miss Casey even when her husband was alive) was bold enough to make any decisive move on the matter. But I knew Father was particularly fond of her. One day as we came home from a town picnic held at the park he told me several times how impressed he had been with Miss Casey's apple pie. For the best-known bakery man in town, I considered his praise of her pie extremely significant.

When Father came home late at night he always left a note with his treat for me. They were notes of simple assurance that everything in this world would be all right, and that the day held no mishap waiting for me and the night should not be feared. The doughnut had become cold just right in the fridge by the time I awoke the next morning. Father used to get up, even though he had barely gone to bed, to make sure everything was all right with me before I started off to school. But a motherless boy learns to take care of himself fast, and by the second year of her absence I became self-sufficient in most things around the house, doing the laundry and making my own school lunches. Gradually Father trusted me enough not to struggle out of his sleep to help me off to school. Most of the time, I could hear him snore in his bedroom as I ate the doughnut with milk and read his note. There is nothing more reassuring for a young boy than the routine and the familiar. He feels safe and comforted by the feeling that everything would always be like this. My home life without Mother was now almost full and always predictable with my father's notes, his doughnuts, and his snoring. Not to disturb his sleep, I would tiptoe out quietly.

Our routine was about as unvarying as the town of Laurinville itself. Aside from unforeseen disasters like Martha, Laurinville had not changed much in the rush of modernization. Its population had remained about the same throughout the years when all other towns seemed to have gained more people. Laurinville's main street had not changed much, except for the repairs carried out after Martha's destruction. In fact, Miss Raynor, the town historian, told me several times during our conversations that Laurinville may be the most unchanged town in modern America. It was so even after the great and terrible desires of the heart that radically altered everything in town for a while.

In the end, Laurinville survived everything—modernization, Martha, and ultimately the Green Palmers. But it almost did not survive the last one.

Chapter Two

Many things change over a period of ten years. People grow older, trees grow taller, and rivers sometimes change their ways. But I can swear my school has not changed all these years. It is still the red-brick, three-building small school it has always been. I can call it "my school" because I was a student there once and now have become one of its few new teachers.

Naturally even most of the teachers are still the same. Mrs. Lucy Wilson, who was my teacher at the time of the Green Palmers, is still there, although only a few years shy of retirement. Her hair is grayer now, almost snow white, and her face somewhat more lined with age, but is the same sweet but stern educator she has always been. Even my father was taught by her and, from the stories he has told me about her, she has hardly changed since my father's time.

The school is located on the south side of Laurinville near the county highway. Its buildings rest on the gently rolling hills, modest in size but comforting with their simplicity. Not too far from the school are the red barns with white trims dotting the farms that surround them.

I sometimes climbed the hills toward the back of the school buildings, to see how far Laurinville stretched. Of course, everyone knows that Laurinville is a small town, but to me at the time it was my whole world. Standing on the highest point of the hills, I could see all of my world, broken only by some more hills, farms, clouds over those hills and farms, bordered by the river that ebbed and flowed with the rainfalls. Farther to the south, our reservoir, which we shared with Atkinson, sometimes reflected the sun like a giant mirror. In the distance, a dark forest formed a circular belt that surrounded Laurinville as if to mark its isolation and boundary from the rest of the world.

Mr. Anderson, a World War II veteran, was the only maintenance man for the entire school. With stooped shoulders and lowered head, he was slow and laborious with every movement that required even a modest bodily exertion. On holidays and graduation days he would wear his uniform, with colorful ribbons and medals that he proudly showed us. The boys were especially impressed with his war heroics. Out of sheer respect for Mr. Anderson it had become our school tradition to help him whenever we could to keep the school clean. Boys and girls volunteered after school hours to help him with his daily maintenance routines, emptying trashcans, sweeping the classrooms, washing windows, cutting the grass, tending the flower gardens on the front of the main building.

The flower gardens have always been the pride and joy of Laurinville. The townspeople volunteered their services to keeping the flowers blooming virtually all year round. The only time that this routine broke down was when the Green Palmers were here. The tradition of students and townspeople helping the school is still continuing with the new maintenance man, Mr. Anderson's son. The new Mr. Anderson took over his father's job after the senior Anderson passed away.

The school was, and still is, run by Mr. LaGrange, the principal, who is actually one of the teachers. He refused, even when told so, to be a full-time administrator. Sitting in his office made him bored, he said, and teaching in the classroom always made him feel young and healthy (although he was only in his early fifties). He even insisted that teachers take days off so that he could teach their classes even when he had his own! With a ruddy, smiling face, he was always a happy and jaunty presence, turning the whole campus into one delightful campground. In concession to his advancing age he has slowed down somewhat lately, I observe, but he is the same wonderful man he has always been.

These images of my school days remain vividly alive in my memory not only because they are still pretty much the same today, but also because they are frozen in my mind as the last images of Laurinville as I remember it before the Green Palmers came. It is human nature, I understand, that one always remembers what one was doing at the time of a particularly traumatic or memorable event. As they are for most people in Laurinville, two things are etched in my mind with a special vividness, the day that Martha killed my mother and the day that the Green Palmers almost destroyed the town's soul. Nothing surrounding these events requires any effort to recall, for they are things that cannot easily be forgotten or quickly replaced by less daunting memories.

The evil that the Green Palmers brought to Laurinville could not have begun with greater uneventfulness. That day had started like any other day. I cannot remember anything special about that day as an harbinger of evil events that were to sweep through our town. I walked to school that day like any other day, greeting the adults that I had known all my childhood and meeting the same friends on the way as I had always done for almost six years. I wish I could say that by some mysterious enlightenment I knew something great and terrible was going to happen to those adults, to my friends, to my town, and

THE GREEN PALMERS

ultimately to myself. But I had no idea that day was going to be any different.

Everything seemed exceedingly normal, except that it was America Day. (We no longer celebrate it because nowadays people are more excited about Constitution Day, which has gradually absorbed many of the America Day celebrations.) As part of our routine, a guest speaker for our class and a field trip to our town library were scheduled.

Mrs. Wilson, who was ordinarily restrained and old-fashioned, had allowed herself to dress brightly for the occasion, with much emphasis on red, white, and blue. Even her hairpins were color coordinated. Still, she looked prim and proper as she always did. I had never seen her untidy in her attire or casual in her manners; even on Sports Day she managed to remain wonderfully dry and well manicured.

Today, sitting on a chair next to her was Mr. Vladimir Yalta, our guest-speaker and the town's only watch repairman, who had years ago immigrated from Russia. He was a man close to sixty, with a gray mustache and wrinkled face, which showed his age and life. He was also one of the subscribers of the Laurinville *Observer*, our three-times-a-week newspaper which I, along with the other boys, delivered. He worked out of a small den in his modest house and once fixed my watch without a charge. He had told me many stories about life in Russia and sang to me many Russian folk songs. He sang his favorite song, "The Volga Boatman," with such a deep voice and emotion that it almost always moved me with feelings. Mrs. Yalta, whose English was still heavy with the Russian accent, often baked cookies for me on my paper route.

"You don't get good cookies from your father," she would say, in particular reference to my father's reputation as an excellent pastry man, and laugh at her own joke. "I am best cookie maker in town."

Judging from the taste of her cookies, her claim often had some basis in truth.

Today Mr. Yalta was dressed in an old suit and a tie, looking extremely formal and proud, as if he could hardly wait his turn to speak. He fidgeted side to side, shifting now and then, and smiling at us with anticipation. He looked at Mrs. Wilson as if asking when the curtain was going to go up. We reacted likewise with an unusually large volume of whispered conversation among ourselves.

"Class," Mrs. Wilson waved us down after the initial commotion had died away, "we have a special guest with us today."

Then she introduced her guest. She said Mr. Yalta had come to America from Russia, which all of us already knew. As a special guest for America Day, she said Mr. Yalta had worn the same suit that he had worn on the day he had been sworn in as a citizen of the United States some twenty years ago. That last fact impressed the class. Expressions of admiration were heard and once again Mrs. Wilson, smiling at Mr. Yalta, waved her hand to quiet us down.

"He is here to tell us what it is like to be an American," she said, "especially for one who, coming from another country, chose to live in the United States of America." She emphasized "another country" and "chose."

After some more routine introduction she motioned Mr. Yalta to come to the front of the class. With a smile, which was as permanent a facial fixture as his eyes, nose and mouth, the guest speaker walked sprightly to the podium to a fairly prolonged hand.

He then began by talking about how he had left Russia to come to America, and telling us some of his early anecdotes of life in a new country. Many of his experiences were humorous and the whole class rocked with laughter. The story of how he learned the meaning of "hotdog," which had nothing to do with either "hot" or "dog," was hilarious. Even Mrs. Wilson, who is very reserved, laughed openly.

Then, in a more serious tone, Mr. Yalta related the difficulties he had encountered in America as a new immigrant. His English was poor and his income meager. But he and Mrs. Yalta struggled to overcome the early difficulties, thanks to the kindness of the many friends they made in Laurinville. Now, he said, he and his wife were the happiest they had ever been in their entire lives. When they died, he said, they would want to be buried in the Laurinville cemetery. This remark about cemetery made me think about my mother. I decided I would take care of their graves, and put fresh flowers there, too.

"But, why?" he suddenly raised his voice to a startled class. "Why did we come to America?"

The class was quiet and expectant.

"Why?" he said again, this time more rhetorically, arching his eyebrows in comic exaggeration, before he answered his own question. "Because of the two things that we did not have in Russia. The two most important things in life in any country." There he paused for effect. Then he put his lips together to make the words as important as he could possibly make them: "Liberty and justice for all."

He whispered the words "liberty" and "justice" as if they were sacred pronouncements that he could not utter without the gravest significance attached to them.

"Liberty and justice for all," Mr. Yalta said once again. "That's why we came to America, and that's what it means to me and my wife to be Americans, believing in liberty and justice for all. Not for some, not for just few, but for everyone. America means liberty and justice are for everyone, or anyone who has come to this country to be free and just. What's liberty without justice? What's justice without liberty? What's liberty and justice if not for everyone? My children, America is the only place in the world where both liberty and justice exist for everyone."

We had said the Pledge of Allegiance many times, which contains those words. But Mr. Yalta made the words sound as if we were hearing them for the first time, or realizing their true meaning for the first time. I could not resist asking him a question.

"Mr. Yalta," I raised my hand. "Why is America the only place in the world where everyone enjoys liberty and justice?"

The guest speaker smiled in appreciation.

"Because in America," he said slowly, "we are always honest with each other, we trust our neighbors, we think about others and not just ourselves, and we love one another and have faith in God. Yes, Mikey, that's why we have liberty and justice for all only in America and why I love Laurinville."

After our guest speaker had finished his speech I could tell that it had left a deep impression upon our minds, especially mine. The words "liberty and justice for all" remained on my mind all throughout the afternoon. They were heard again during our field trip to the library. Mrs. Raynor, who did double duty as a librarian, showed many of the Constitutional documents and explained their significance.

Liberty and justice for all. Important though they may be, to most boys my age such words represented only a relatively short, passing interest. Were it not for the events that soon followed, therefore, these words would have also lost their significance in no time. But fate brought together those words, the Green Palmers, and my own role in a confrontation not to be easily forgotten.

But, as I was leaving the campus, I found myself still muttering those words in all innocence, oblivious to the coming shadows of evil. At least for the moment, I felt there were no words more important than those five words: Liberty and justice for all.

Chapter Three

The Laurinville *Observer* is like any other small-town newspaper.

The emphasis should be on small and town. It is mostly about small announcements like birthdays, weddings, births and deaths, and town meetings and picnics. It is entirely understandable that most townspeople take their newspaper in stride, paying only cursory attention to the goings on. Most of what is printed in the paper is old news to them, for they have already heard the "news" through grapevines. The only time the town read the paper with any special interest was when, a few years ago, Laurinville got involved in a small disagreement with its next-door town, Atkinson, over water supply. The problem was soon resolved peacefully, and the *Observer* had a hand in settling the dispute. For that role the mayor of Laurinville gave the paper the "Peacemaker of the Year" award, which greatly embarrassed the *Observer*.

Even today the *Observer* continues to be a small-town newspaper without much change. Jamie Yarborough, my former babysitter, now works full time for the paper's small advertising department. In fact, she is the whole department. Such is the size of business for the newspaper.

I, along with a few other boys, made up the regular delivery corps for the paper, which came out on Mondays, Wednesdays, and Fridays. The only time this schedule varied, but only briefly, was during the water dispute. My route took about two hours to complete and much of it was spent talking to the subscribers. The money I earned from the paper route was put away for college at the only bank in town. Most other boys in the delivery corps did likewise. We were in a similar age group and were good friends, often covering one another's route on emergencies. Sometimes their parents volunteered to help us out.

The school and the newspaper office, such as it was, were on the same side of Laurinville, separated by a county highway which, with two other much smaller and less traveled roads, connected the town to the outside world. It was on this county highway that the town's only billboard—it seems there was only one of anything in Laurinville—stood. On the side facing the incoming traffic was normally the town's greetings to the visitors: "WELCOME TO LAURINVILLE. HOME OF . POPULATION," etc., etc. (Now, the town motto, "Liberty and Justice for All," has been added to the greetings.) The other side of the billboard facing the town most often stayed unoccupied simply because there was no reason for anyone to advertise. If there was anything to advertise, the townspeople already knew about it. Grapevine exchanges of information and happenings were still the fastest and most reliable means by which news traveled throughout Laurinville. The corps of paperboys made up the best network of news-gatherers, normally getting the announcements from their subscribers, which then appeared in the paper somewhat later.

Today, as I was walking past the billboard on my way to the *Observer* to do my afternoon delivery, I saw a man hunched over on the scaffold on the side of the billboard facing the town, trying to paste a large poster on it. The man had on a pair of white painters' overalls as if he had been doing the work all day.

I did not recognize him as someone from Laurinville. Since I had seldom seen the billboard used for anything, I stood nearby in mild curiosity watching the man complete his work. The slight breeze of the afternoon, blowing the large paper this way and that, made his work somewhat difficult at times. In a manner that suggested professional experience, however, the man finished his work in due time. He climbed down the ladder, stepped back from the billboard, and inspected it for a few seconds. Apparently satisfied, he acknowledged my presence and nodded.

I stood there looking at the picture on the billboard, fascinated. It was startling for its simplicity. There was only one picture in the middle of the large white poster. It was the palm of a hand raised as if to say "stop, and take a look at me." What was even more fascinating was the fact that the palm was colored dark green in white background. It was a green palm. Below the green palm was a caption in bold black: "COMING SOON. GREEN PALM SEMINARS." There were no other words or signs.

Green Palm Seminars? I was positively puzzled and curious.

"What's Green Palm Seminars?" I asked the man who was now gathering his belongings onto a small truck parked on the side. He carried the ladder as his last item and loaded in onto the vehicle and put up the tailgate.

"Some kind of safety classes?" I said while the man was still busy. "We have them at school. Mr. LaGrange taught us how to save life."

"I don't know, son," the man said. "I only put them up as they tell me to. I put up many more of those in Atkinson this morning."

With that, the man got into his truck and drove away.

I stood there for the next few minutes, trying to figure out what that green palm could mean. The word seminar vaguely suggested a gathering of professors talking about something nobody else understood. If I had been endowed with any clairvoyance or even a few years older, I might have been struck by the coincidence of the two very strong events that afternoon: Mr. Yalta's liberty-and-justice speech and the green palm seminars.

Of course, I didn't know then that a twelve-year old boy of no great significance was about to be thrust upon the crossroads where the two ideas intersected and, in retrospect, even clashed violently with each other.

Somehow transfixed by what I was seeing and vaguely disturbed by my own unfathomable reaction to it all, I stood there watching the billboard and then the truck which was now disappearing from view. Clouds of darker hues hovered over the end of the road where the truck slid over the last hill in the direction of Atkinson.

I had barely forgotten about the green palm seminars when I got to the newspaper office. There my mind received another jolt. On the bottom half of the *Observer's* front page was the same green palm, this time without the color green because the *Observer* had no color capacity yet, and the announcement about the upcoming green palm seminars. There was no more explanation in the newspaper than what was on the billboard. I thought about asking Jamie, who might still be in her back office there, about the green palm seminars in case she knew something about them. But I was already behind my usual schedule, on the account that I had spent some time at the site of the billboard, and decided not to bother with the matter.

The delivery route was uneventful. As usual on a day when rain was expected, I walked into the houses and left the paper inside. People in Laurinville, then as today, rarely locked the doors. Mr. Yalta in his work clothes, busily looking through his magnifying glass at a small ladies' watch, waved at me when I stopped by. His workroom as usual was full of old watches, some whole and many with parts missing. There were tiny screws, coils, springs, and boxes of every conceivable tool and part laying all around him. On the wall to his right was a large poster of a pocket watch showing all its parts separated from the frame but connected with straight lines, indicating where the parts belonged in the watch. Not surprisingly, Mrs. Yalta held two cookies of considerable size, still warm, wrapped in a napkin for me.

But as I turned to go Mr. Yalta called to me. I stopped and turned around, part of a cookie still in my mouth.

"Mikey," he said with his usual smile, rising from his work chair, "I have something special for you. You can carry it with you since you don't have too much more to go with your route."

He reached down under his worktable and pulled out a flat cardboard box large enough for me to stand under in case of rain. In fact, that was the thought that had first entered my mind when I saw the box and I felt immediately ashamed of myself. He came out of his office and handed it to me. I accepted it uncertainly. It did not weigh much in my hands.

"What is it, Mr. Yalta?" I said, still uncertain. Playfully I shook it to see if I could guess what could be inside. For a twelve-year old boy, curiosity was killing.

"Something I made specially for you," he said, knowing in satisfaction that he had aroused my curiosity. "Just take it home and open it."

For the rest of the route I kept the package securely tucked under my arm, still trying to guess. After a while I gave up.

Mrs. Mary Blake, the widow of the former mayor of Laurinville, who had died heroically during the tornado trying to save its citizens (his statue has also been erected), paid me her subscription dues in advance and gave me a quarter as she often did. Many others among the subscribers also paid their dues during my route. Like Mrs. Blake, a few of them gave me a quarter as it was their usual custom. Some of them left extra instructions for me to do, such as feeding their pets and watering their plants if they had to go away long. These subscribers were especially generous with their gift toward my college. On that day, virtually all of them frowned in puzzlement when they saw the palm on the front page.

Despite the threatening rain I stopped by the bank on the way home to unload the money. The teller helped me count the small changes I had and duly recorded it in my book. She offered me candy but I had to decline. As I was leaving the bank after completing my transaction Mr. McNamee, the banker, came out of his corner office and motioned me to come back. Mr. McNamee was a tall and skinny man in his early forties whose few wispy strands of hair on his head always threatened to block his vision. His son Greg was in my class and I sometimes spent nights with him at his home. The McNamees lived in a modest house, much like ours. He always said that the banker had no right to live any better than those who trusted him and deposited their money in his bank. Honest and considerate, he was naturally one of the leading citizens of Laurinville.

I followed the banker into his office. On his desk was my bankbook in which the deposits were recorded. He asked me about my father and my school. But he knew that I was anxious to get back home before the rain started.

"All right, Mikey," he said with a smile. "I am happy to tell you that your college fund is much bigger than both you and I thought."

I said I didn't understand him.

"We just discovered a mistake," Mr. McNamee said. "You have much more money in your account than we previously believed."

He opened my bankbook and showed me where the mistake had occurred. It was not a large amount. Apparently it was a mistake that could have easily been overlooked. But Mr. McNamee's bank would not overlook even the smallest error on its part. Like the other businesses in Laurinville, the bank was absolutely scrupulous. Somewhat delighted with the discovery, I thanked him and turned to leave his office. Then a thought occurred to me.

"Mr. McNamee," I said, thinking since he was a banker he might know something about it, "do you know what a green palm seminar is?"

The banker frowned and pointed to the *Observer* that had just been delivered to him, and shook his head.

"No idea, Mikey," he said. "I've never heard of them before. But I will see what I can find out."

I hurried home from the bank, clutching the package that Mr. Yalta had given me, afraid it could be rained on and anxious to know what was in it. But, after all, the clouds were a false alarm. The rain did not come. For almost a month now, no rain had fallen in the Laurinville area. I vaguely remembered that people were a bit worried about the decreasing volume of water in the reservoir, which also affected Atkinson.

Rushing to my upstairs room I opened the box. Carefully wrapped inside was a beautiful picture frame. But, instead of a picture, there was an inscription on a white canvas. In bold black Roman letters, like those writings on the face of a precious watch, and meticulously done by Mr. Yalta's own hand, the inscription simply said:

LIBERTY AND JUSTICE FOR ALL

I stared at the inscription in silence, almost without breathing. They were familiar words. I heard and spoke them myself many times before. I could recite the whole Pledge even in my sleep. But for some reason those words looked different today. Not only was it because Mr. Yalta gave a speech about their meaning in celebration of America Day, but also because his gift suddenly and inexplicably reminded me of the green palm I had seen. Both demanded attention and were strikingly similar in their simplicity of presentation. One simply said "LIBERTY AND JUSTICE FOR ALL" without embellishment in white background. The other, likewise, only showed a green palm with the caption, "COMING SOON. GREEN PALM SEMINARS."

I looked at the gift but my thought returned to the green palm. I was looking at the familiar words but I was thinking about the strange green palm. After a while, tired from the effort of trying to connect two things that seemed to have nothing in common with each other, I gave up both activities.

Not being able to decide where to hang Mr. Yalta's laborious handiwork I stood it against the wall next to my bed. When I went to bed that night I found myself staring at it again. The inscription and the green palm were still on my mind as I fell asleep.

The next day at school the main topic of conversation was the upcoming green palm seminars. Life in Laurinville had been so predictable and uneventful that even a minor curiosity caused a stir in speculation. But, not surprisingly, no one seemed to know what they were all about. Greg McNamee reported that even his father had failed to find out anything about the green palm. Naturally all sorts of speculation were invented. Some even suggested that the green palm actually belonged to the Martians who were coming to Laurinville to make everyone a Martian. This suggestion invited a round of Martian imitations among the boys.

We shouted, "The Martians are coming! The Martians are coming!" and chased each other, making grotesque faces with our eyes and tongues. Of course, the green palm had nothing to do with the Martians. But, as it turned out, it was a phenomenon just as strange and terrifying as the invasion of the phantom Martians.

Chapter Four

The next few days passed without any special event. However, two minor phenomena continued to puzzle many people and irritate some just under the skin.

One was obviously the dry spell that forecast no relief anytime soon. The always thoughtful mayor of Laurinville, Mr. Robin Miller, a reluctant leader who really didn't want to be mayor or anything with heavy responsibility, began to mention the possibility for water restrictions. The mayor's office in Laurinville has always been a voluntary position which has gone to the most respected citizen in town. In this fine tradition of civic leadership, Mr. Miller decided to let everyone know that he rinsed his mouth only twice when he brushed his teeth. By letting out even this small information, he hoped that the townspeople would pick up on it. Indeed, people soon caught on to the mayor's message and started restricting their water consumption. As in most other things in Laurinville, this water conservation was put into effect in a perfectly voluntary spirit among its citizens and no one complained.

The other phenomenon was likewise low-keyed in its existence, just beneath the surface, with people thinking about it only in their own minds. It was the puzzling "green palm seminar" which promised to come to Laurinville. As days passed following the appearance of the green palm on the billboard and in the *Observer*, people began to openly speculate on what it could possibly be. When I delivered the newspaper I noticed people quickly glancing at the front page. Not finding anything there, they would go through the rest of the paper apparently looking for more on the green palm seminar. This was all the more noticeable to me because they were trying to appear nonchalant and inconspicuous about their curiosity. Even my father mentioned it once in obviously pretended passing. The normally placid air in our town was suddenly thick with unanswered speculation and unspoken curiosity. It seemed everyone was dying to know what it was but no one was willing to mention it openly.

The answer to the "green palm seminars"—though none to the dry spell—came exactly a week later. The announcement occupied, again, the bottom half of the *Observer*'s front page. In bold letters, the following paragraphs appeared under the palm logo:

CITIZENS OF LAURINVILLE!

THE GREEN PALMERS ARE COMING! THE GREEN PALMERS ARE COMING!

THEY ARE COMING TO SPREAD THE "GREEN PALM WAY OF LIFE." WHAT IS THE GREEN PALM WAY? IT'S SIMPLE. IT'S EASY WEALTH AND SHINING FORTUNE FOR THE MOST IMPORTANT PERSON IN YOUR LIFE. WHICH IS YOU. YES, YOU! WEALTH AND FORTUNE FOR YOU, JUST FOR YOU!

WHY STRUGGLE SO HARD AT THE BOTTOM WHEN YOU CAN GET TO THE TOP EASY AND

FAST?
WHY ONLY ENVY OTHER PEOPLE WHEN YOU CAN HAVE EVERYTHING YOU ALWAYS WANTED?
WHY PUT OFF UNTIL ANOTHER DAY WHAT YOU CAN HAVE TODAY?
WHY WAIT UNTIL ANOTHER LIFE WHEN YOU LIVE ONLY ONCE?

THE ANSWER IS SIMPLE: WEALTH AND FORTUNE FOR YOU. AND NOBODY ELSE. NOW, NOT LATER.

WEALTH AND FORTUNE FOR YOURSELF, BY YOURSELF, AND OF YOURSELF SHALL ALWAYS BE THE GREEN PALM WAY OF LIFE, etc., etc.

Emphasizing "wealth," "fortune," and "yourself," the advertisement then went on to promise that the green palm seminars were offered for a modest fee to anyone who wanted to achieve his long-deserved wealth and fortune in life. It also quoted people obviously from other towns who swore that the seminars had helped achieve their own easy wealth and shining fortune. There were some famous names that even I could recognize. Under these testimonials was a phrase in small print that said, "compensated endorsement" which I didn't understand. The seminar, first in a series, would be offered that Saturday at the school auditorium, which was the only place in town large enough to hold a public meeting.

I must confess that the advertisement made no great impression on me. Having anticipated something more exciting from the green palm suspense I suffered a twinge of disappointment. I remember talking to myself when I read it for the first time, "Gee, is that all?" What is now known as "green palmism" elsewhere in the world was completely new to Laurinville and certainly new to me. Mrs. Wilson, who taught social studies, had never mentioned green palmism to us before. If she had not mentioned it to us, it could not have been important. The boys at school expressed the same disappointment at the green palm and tried to find something else to occupy their minds.

But reactions of the adults were different. They were now hungrily waiting for the newspaper. I had never seen them so eager to read the paper since the water incident with Atkinson. Most of them were quiet and serious as they read the advertisement. Mr. Yalta, obviously more agitated than the others, shook his head vigorously and said something to his wife in Russian, pointing to the newspaper. Mrs. Yalta was so absorbed in her husband's comment that she forgot to give me the cookies she held in her hand. Mrs. Blake, the hero's widow, upon getting the paper from me and reading the section, quietly withdrew into her house and closed the door.

I found Miss Casey, one of the last on my route, working on her own car on the driveway. She greeted me happily, wading through the tools and parts of her car strewn all over the driveway, and hugged me.

"I decided to work on my own car for a change," she said, explaining why she was home early. "So, what's new in the newspaper, Mikey?"

Somewhat puzzled by the reactions to the advertisement I had been witnessing, I just handed her the paper without comment. Miss Casey, sensing something unusual, sat down on the driveway and read the front page quickly. Then looking up at me she went back to reading it for the second time, this time more slowly.

"The Green Palm Way of Life, uh?" she repeated the words a couple of times. "So, they are offering you all the wealth and fortune you deserve…" When I said nothing, she quoted some parts from the message to herself. Then she fell into thoughtful silence.

"Well, who needs wealth and fortune?" I said, for some reason feeling defiant. "My dad brings me doughnuts every night."

Miss Casey smiled at my brave response. Then she said to herself again, "So, the Green Palmers are coming. They are coming to save us from all our pain and unhappiness."

"Are you going?" I asked.

"Going where?"

"You know, the seminar this Saturday."

She slowly shook her head and said no, she didn't think she would. "They are wrong," she said those words softly as if to herself. "They are absolutely wrong…"

I did not understand the meaning of her comments at all. My ignorance about the whole Green Palm affair forced Miss Casey to change the subject. She suggested that I help her with her car and she would fix me a nice sandwich after that. I agreed.

After delivering the rest of the papers I returned to her house and to learn more about car repairs. For the next hour or so we stayed busy with something more practical. However, I could sense that a part of Miss Casey's mind was still on the Green Palmers. Now and then she fell silent and then shook her head as if answering her own silent questions. Miss Casey fixed us a sandwich and a bowl of soup each when we were done with her car. The cool breeze in the quiet of late afternoon made for a pleasant snack time for us as we sat on the grass and munched our food. That moment of happiness made me forget all about the green palm's puzzling effect on the townspeople. Miss Casey offered to take me fishing that Saturday. I said I would be happy to go fishing with her if Father had no objections.

The next morning when I was getting ready to go to school I saw the front page of the paper on the kitchen table. Normally Father would have glanced over it quickly when he got home and disposed of in a box where we collected paper trash separately from the rest. Father and I had always had such regular habits that even seeing the paper still on the table seemed odd. Its front page advertisement for the Green Palm Way almost made my heart jump. Something else was unusual. It was the note that always accompanied the doughnuts. Father would scribble something on a piece of paper, mostly routine stuff like "enjoy your treat, from the best bakery man in Laurinville." This he had never missed. But the note was not there this morning. I even searched the bottom of the fridge for the missing note. A father forgetting to write a note to his son may not be unusual even by the Laurinville standard. But this was the first time in my memory that my otherwise meticulous father had forgotten something so routine.

Something seemed odd. Perhaps it was the newspaper still on the table. Perhaps it was all the subtle reactions to the newspaper that I had seen in people the day before. Individually, these things meant nothing significant. Together, they created a strange but undefinable effect. But, still, it was nothing more disturbing than not seeing your dog coming out to meet you when you come home. Whatever it might have been, the absent note from my father impressed upon me enough to remember the incident all day.

After a while no one at school mentioned the Green Palmers,

as they were now called. They held no more fascination for my schoolmates than did the Martians. The Green Palmers' offer of wealth and fortune meant very little to us. After all, the way of life in Laurinville was mostly in farming and small crafts, people doing their day's work for their day's wages and livelihood. So no one was so wealthy enough and no one was so poor enough to pay particular attention to the issue. Soon I also forgot all about the Green Palmers—and the missing note from Father—for the rest of the day.

That evening I hung Mr. Yalta's present on the wall just above the headboard of my bed. I felt a small measure of satisfaction when, after several tries, I finally got the frame perfectly balanced. It was going to be a surprise for Father when he saw it. However, that satisfaction was dashed quickly when I found the newspaper in the trash container—with the Green Palmer's message cut out. For some unknown reason, my heart pounded for a few seconds. It was as if someone or something had intruded upon our happy family, ruining the fine routines of our life. It was more annoying than anything, for then I had no knowledge of the enormity of things to come to our life and to our town.

I remember wondering what possible use my father could have ever found in that silly offer of wealth and fortune.

Chapter Five

With Father's permission I went fishing with Miss Casey all day Saturday.

Not only was she a first-class auto-mechanic, she was also a superb bass fisherman. The small pond belonged to a grateful customer of Miss Casey's automotive genius, who had urged her to come and enjoy the fishing before the water dried up in the continuing drought.

We had driven about a mile off the main road, passing a small white church which she pointed out was her church, then further on a dirt road to reach the pond. It was surrounded by grassy pastures upon which a few cows, their tails lazily chasing the flies, were grazing. Although it was quite early in the morning, the night's dewdrops had already begun to dry up under the brilliant morning sun. It was going to be another bright and, unhappily for most people in Laurinville, dry day. Nearby fields, crops ready to be harvested, stretched in all directions as far as the belt of the dark forest that marked the boundary for Laurinville.

The water level had gone down considerably during the drought. We could see the different water marks on the clay banks as the level decreased each day. The smaller volume of water made me a respectable fisherman too, as I happily reeled in some three-pounders myself. I had gone fishing a few times before with Father but each experience of pulling in a fish was always as thrilling as if it was the very first time. Miss Casey said she was planning a big fish fry to which she would invite Father and me. When I took the opportunity and told her how complimentary Father had been about her apple pie, she blushed to deep purple.

In between the catches we ate our sandwiches and talked mostly about the two things that seemed to be on everyone's mind: The drought and the Green Palmers. But neither subject yielded much substance to our speculation. There was so little we could do about the first subject, and so little we knew about the second. We soon got tired of talking about either of them. The day was breezy with Indian summer's laziness and balm, and the fishing was good. And I loved Miss Casey. The possibility of her and my father getting married was so exciting that the very idea itself made me smile goofy smiles.

"What are you smiling about, Mikey?" Miss Casey would ask, catching me in one of my private thoughts.

I just said "nothing" and concentrated on fishing.

At the end of the day my fishing companion dropped me off at home and drove off. As I walked in I was so surprised to see Father still at home that I almost let out a small cry.

"Dad," I said, "why aren't you at work?"

"I called in sick, son," Father said without looking at me.

"But, you are not sick, are you, Dad?" I asked, alarmed.

"No, I am not," Father said.

"But, then, why…?"

"I didn't feel like going to work today, son," he said with slight irritation. "Besides, you have to use up your sick days, or else you just let them go to waste." Father said it in such a way that seemed to discourage any further inquiry from his son.

I wanted to protest that he had always enjoyed working and had never called in sick when he wasn't actually too sick to go to work. That happened only twice in my life time that I could remember. Both times Father had been really sick. What was wrong this time? I wondered.

"I am tired of working all the time," Father said, as if reading the silent question in my mind. Then he switched the subject and asked me how the fishing had gone. I got excited about my fishing expedition and told him how many bass I had caught. I also mentioned that Miss Casey was going to give us a fish fry soon. The mention of Miss Casey's name seemed to brighten Father's face briefly, but only briefly. He went back to his utterly serious face that I had seldom seen, not even when we were at the cemetery for Mother. Something in my father's manner disturbed me. We had been so close, for so long, that much of our communication was done on instinct. Now, I instinctively felt that he was hiding something from me.

Then I noticed something on the table in front of him. It was a glossy brochure with colorful pictures of men and women in various stages of pleasure registered on their faces. On the cover was a title across the top: "HOW TO BE A GREEN PALMER: AN INTRODUCTION TO THE GREEN PALM WAY OF LIFE."

So, after all, Father had been to the Green Palmer Seminar!

I asked him about the seminar and what the Green Palmers had told him there, but Father said very little in response. It was the first time in my memory that Father had failed to satisfy my curiosity. After some further unsuccessful tries, I excused myself and went upstairs, saying that I needed to get my homework done. As I was going up the steps, I could hear Father opening up the brochure, the introductory manual for the Green Palmers.

Unhappiness swept over me once I got in my room. I was unhappy but I didn't know why I was unhappy. The day with

Miss Casey had been wonderful, and the fishing great. But my father's solemn face and his refusal to be forthright about the seminar worried me. I had no clear idea about the Green Palmers but their effect on my father was at the center of my unhappiness. Even as I stared at Mr. Yalta's handiwork on the wall, the picture of the green palm kept coming in front of the words, "liberty and justice for all."

Apparently Father was reading the Green Palmer manual in the kitchen. I heard the pages turn and the chair squeak at a fairly regular interval. I tried to do some homework of my own but found it difficult to concentrate. Disturbed and unhappy, and tired from the day of outdoor activity, I fell asleep to a series of dreams that I could remember only vaguely.

One of the dreams that I did remember was about strange men, none from Laurinville, taking my father into a building while I was desperately trying to hold onto him. I tried to holler but, as it usually is in dreams, no sound came out. It was only when the men suddenly noticed something written on the wall that they let go of Father and disappeared. When I turned to the wall to see what had scared them away, I saw "LIBERTY AND JUSTICE FOR ALL" written in impressively huge letters. All I could think was, when did Mr. Yalta have the time to write it there?

I was startled out of my dreams when Father called from downstairs to tell me that dinner was ready. For a few seconds I was disoriented, not knowing where I was. I regained my consciousness by staggering to the bathroom and throwing some cold water on my face. I was relieved that it was all a dream. Instantly the dream was forgotten.

Father was waiting for me with food on the table. He seemed to be in a better mood than before and tried to joke with me as we started eating. I remained silent.

"Listen to this," he said almost to himself, pointing to the Green Palmer's manual which was opened to a page that he apparently had been reading. "'The risk-free investment into venture capital gains is an excellent idea for maximum quarterly yields and guaranteed profits.'"

He might as well have said it to himself because I had no idea what he was talking about. I had never heard "risk-free investment," "venture capital gains," "quarterly yields," or "guaranteed profits" before in my life. Father went on some more with the manual but it all sounded like a foreign language to me. He read several more sections from the manual, which seemed to have particularly interested him. All throughout they frequently referred to "wealth" and "fortune," which were obviously what the Green Palm Way was all about.

I was relieved that Father seemed to have regained his normal self, but could not help feeling that there was something odd about his animated happiness. He was loud and silly like the king in a fairy tale, and unlike the normally quiet and patient man he had always been. And I didn't like the changes in him.

My uneasiness with Father did not improve the next day when he announced that we were not going to the cemetery to do our weekly cleaning and changing flowers for Mother. He said the weather had been dry and there could not be anything there to clean up.

"What about the flowers, Dad?" I cried in disbelief.

"They will last another week," he said. "Well, perhaps we should get artificial flowers for her. They last much longer and cost much less."

I had never heard Father talk like that before and had to sit down on a chair, ready to cry. "Well, son," he said kindly in an obvious effort to calm me down. "If it makes you feel better, you can go there by yourself."

"But why don't you want to go, Dad?" I pleaded with him. "You don't have anything else to do."

He eyed the Green Palmer's manual and said, "I've got to read some more of that stuff. It's important."

I pleaded with him some more but it was no use. He was determined not to budge. So I ended up going to Mother's cemetery alone for the first time in my memory. I stopped at Mr. Dixon's store for some flowers on the way to the cemetery. Father was right about the weather having kept the place clean. There wasn't much cleaning to do. But by habit I swept the whole site with the small broom that I had brought with me and changed the flowers.

Here and there I saw several other families also doing theirs for their loved ones. When some of them came by and asked why I was there alone, I almost burst out crying. I told them Father wasn't feeling too well. However, having to lie like that made me extremely unhappy with my father. Once I was alone at the cemetery after the others left, I finally broke down and cried. For the first time in my life I felt lonely, and the cemetery, which had always given me comfort, appeared solitary and deserted. For a brief moment my woes and sorrows were interrupted by a squirrel in search of food that came close to where I was sitting. I watched the animal hop from spot to spot and then climb up a tree nearby all the way to the top, and hopping to another treetop and another treetop until I could not see it any more. Its disappearance thus ending my temporary fascination, I was brought back to my present woes and sorrows and to shedding some more tears. After a while I stopped crying and, picking up my broom and the old flowers, walked back home still feeling miserable.

The next day was Monday and I was expecting as usual to lead the class in the Pledge of Allegiance. But Mrs. Wilson, looking tired and not in her usual sprightly form, told the class that we would suspend the Pledge for a while.

"Doing it too much makes it meaningless," she said to a rather surprised class. "Perhaps we should do it once a month or so."

As always on Mondays she collected our homework assignments, which she took home with her to grade. But today she proceeded to give us some reading to do as, she said, she wanted to grade our homework in class.

"I have some reading to do myself at home," she told a still surprised class. "From now on, I will grade your homework in class to save my time."

She then put on her glasses and started going through our homework. Mrs. Wilson looked somewhat tired and distracted as if she had been up all night. As everyone started reading the assignment, I found myself observing our teacher. She yawned a couple of times, which in itself was startling, for we had never seen her do that before. Her glasses dropped down on her nose frequently. For the rest of the day Mrs. Wilson's class was generally listless and slow. It was only when the bell rang for lunch recess that she seemed positively relieved and came alive. Greg agreed with me during lunch and concluded that Mrs. Wilson must not be feeling well. This observation somehow reminded me of Father the day before.

Many unusual, surprising things were happening in my life. But they were so random and insignificant that I could not connect them into any pattern or explanation. I could react to only one thing at a time.

More disturbing still was what lay ahead.

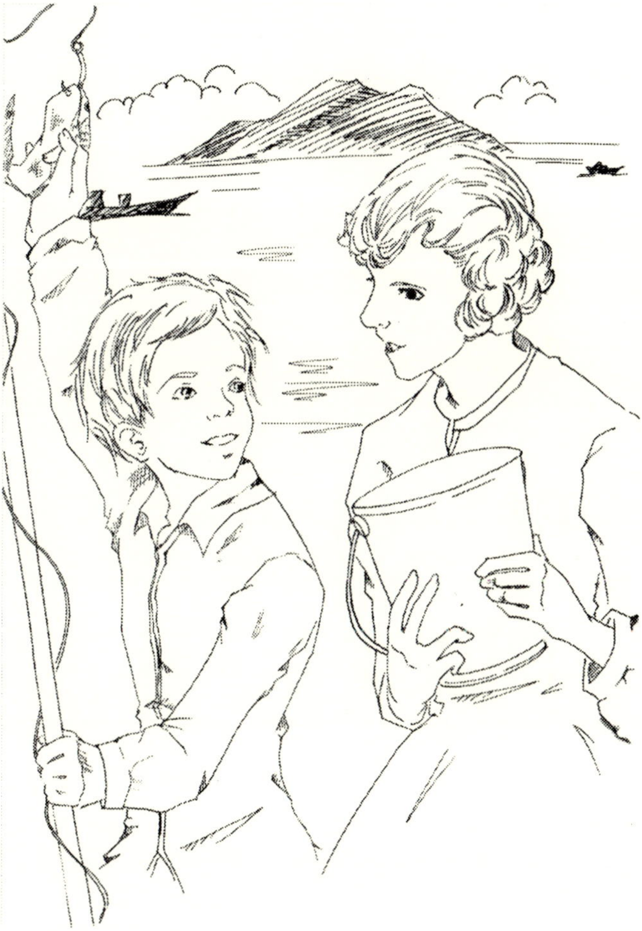

Chapter Six

During my paper route certain things, never before observed in Laurinville, happened.

A few subscribers who paid me in cash for the *Observer* insisted that I count the money to make sure it was correct. When I said it wasn't necessary as I had never done it before, many of them said something like, "I would count it if I were you." I thought it strange that people suddenly seemed so nervous.

I also noticed that people at several houses were putting in deadbolt locks on their doors. Mr. Rogers was the third such house that I encountered.

Mr. Rogers was Laurinville's police chief who also doubled as his own deputy, receptionist, ambulance driver, and dispatcher, all while working as a full-time electrician. "For insurance purpose, Mikey," he said, responding to my surprised look. "We just got the notice to do this. I guess you can't be too sure about things nowadays." He muttered the last part of his statement almost to himself as he went back to putting the lock together.

I also noticed that he was wearing his gunbelt, although the holster was empty. The only time he had ever worn his gun was during the America Day parade when the celebration was more vigorously than now. The gun had always been strictly ceremonial and, as far as we knew, it was fired just once for the purpose of celebration. In fact, we were surprised that Mr. Rogers knew how to fire it. But seeing the gunbelt on the chief today I almost reminded him that there was no parade forthcoming that I knew of.

I told him that I had seen two more houses on my route with new deadbolt locks being installed. That information did not seem to surprise the chief.

"Yeah, a lot of that's going on around here now," he said as he was tightening the screws on the lock. "I couldn't get into a house this morning to fix an electrical short. The family forgot to tell me they had just put in a deadbolt lock on their door."

A similar development at Mrs. Blake's house was taking place, but on a slightly larger scale. There were two workmen from Atkinson (I could tell by the logo on their back) who were putting up metal bars on her front window. Another man was drilling a hole on the door frame with the obvious intention of putting in a new lock. A box that contained a deadbolt lock, one similar to Mr. Rogers's, lay on the floor. The hero's widow was in her house robe directing the men. She was telling them to secure the bars tightly as she actually pulled on one to test it.

"How are you, Mrs. Blake?" I greeted her cheerfully as I handed her the paper. She had always been one of my favorite subscribers.

The normally sweet Mrs. Blake frowned and whispered, "not good."

"What's going on here?" I inquired, pointing to the busy scene with my head.

"It's not safe to be without protection," she said. "They don't know I live on widows' pension, which has been generous enough, thanks to Laurinville."

"What are you talking about? Who are *they*?"

"You know, *them*," she whispered again. As she was about

to say more one of the men working on the bars called to her for further instruction with their work. The hero's widow waved me goodbye as she walked toward the men.

I stood there for a few seconds collecting my thoughts before moving on.

The scene at Mr. Shepeck's household, however, was much more interesting to me. Mr. Shepeck, Laurinville's only funeral director and barber, a small man with thinning dark hair falling all over his head, was trying to tame a huge dog, assisted by his daughter, Amber, who was in my class. They were trying to make the dog obey their commands, which they were reading from a small book. But the new member of the family was in no mood to cooperate, straining at the leash which threatened to break any moment. I got into the spirit of their struggle. Throwing my paper satchel down on the grass, I joined their training session for the next thirty minutes or so. Finally, at the end there was a semblance of obedience in that huge animal. At least he managed to sit and bark on command. He, now named "Spotty" (apparently for his dark brown spots), seemed to be more fond of Amber; or at least he obeyed her commands more readily than mine or Mr. Shepeck's.

"He is a big dog. Where did you get him, Mr. Shepeck?" I asked as we all stood there wiping our brows.

"Oh, from a vet I know in Atkinson, who breeds guard dogs on the side."

"Guard dogs?"

"Yes," the funeral director-barber said, stroking Spotty's head, "he will scare away any potential thief."

"I didn't know you needed a guard dog," I said uncertainly. "We hardly…"

"Well, you never know," Mr. Shepeck said, looking around him somewhat suspiciously. "Better to be safe than sorry."

To my knowledge no one in Laurinville ever had a dog for anything other than as a house pet. But I did not mention it to Mr. Shepeck who obviously felt in need of a guard dog and was happy with what he found. Spotty made me want to have a dog of my own. I thought about asking Father to get me one. We had a dog once, but after it was killed in a hunting accident we thought no more about getting another one.

However, thinking about Father somehow made me feel less than comfortable. This feeling about him was in itself a new experience for me. Father had always been nothing other than Father, patient, steady, and predictable. But now, I felt as if I were the orphan that I had read about in a story book who was about to be sent to a new place, leaving the ones he knew and loved. He had his bag packed and, driven there by an inconsiderate cab driver, he was about to ring the doorbell of a very unfriendly orphanage. Anxiety and uncertainty had invaded my small boy's heart, which had known nothing but happiness and security in Laurinville.

I found Mr. Yalta deep in thought, holding in his hand what appeared to be an official letter. I approached him to hand over the paper and thanked him for his present. He was so absorbed in reading the letter that he merely nodded his head in recognizing me and my greetings.

"Hand delivered from the mayor's office just a few minutes ago," Mr. Yalta said almost to himself. "Hmmmmm, I don't know why they are starting this now."

Something in his reaction made me bold. "What is it, Mr. Yalta?" I inquired.

The watch repairman from Russia looked up at me and shook the letter.

"Well, Mikey—" he stumbled with my name as if he had forgotten who I was for a moment, "the town office wants me to register my business for, it reads, 'licensing administration and revenue purposes.'"

"What does that mean? Licen…"

"I don't know," Mr. Yalta said scratching his head. "I guess they want me to pay taxes on my watch repairs. I have been repairing watches for twenty years in Laurinville but this is the first time anything like this was required."

"Does that mean you have to pay?"

"I guess so," he said, "and have to get a license to fix watches. I guess it had to come, yes, sir, it had to come."

He repeated "it had to come" several times to himself, and absent-mindedly went back to work. Very unusual for him, he even forgot that I was still standing there.

During the rest of the route my mind kept hearing Mr. Yalta's muttering, "it had to come, it had to come." I was hoping to see Miss Casey at her house to talk to her, but she was not there.

Somewhat disappointed and lonely, I was walking back home when I found a twenty-dollar bill lodged in the crack on the pavement. It was folded two ways and with ink smudges in one corner. Mr. Rogers's house, which was also Laurinville's police station, was too far to walk back to. Deciding to turn it in on the way to school the next day, I put the money in my pocket and trudged home.

Father was getting ready to go to work when I got home. I told him what I had seen on my paper route and asked him if we could get a dog, not a big grownup dog but a small puppy.

"Oh?" he said noncommittally. "Let's think about it."

He became thoughtful when I told him about the deadbolt locks and bars people were putting in. He said something like, "maybe we should have those things put in, too."

When I mentioned the twenty-dollar bill I had found, Father

THE GREEN PALMERS

volunteered to take it to the police chief on the way to work. I pulled out the money and handed it over to him. It was still folded the way I had found it. Father stretched out his right hand to receive it.

That's when I first noticed it. His palm was pale green.

"Dad," I said, looking at his palm, forgetting about the money. "The color on your palm. It's green!"

"Yes, it is, isn't it?" he said, taking the money and putting it in his pocket. He then looked at both his palms, which were equally green. He rubbed them together as if to make the color disappear that way.

"Food coloring?" I asked, wondering what kind of doughnuts or pastries could have required green coloring.

"Maybe," Father said, "I wouldn't worry about it."

With that he left for work. I did not worry about it. For a man who handled gobs of food coloring it was not unusual to have colored palms for a while.

It never occurred to me, even for a moment, to think of Father's palm as a Green Palm.

Chapter Seven

The following week, while the Green Palm Seminars were offered almost every day, several odd events took place.

Event number one was Greg McNamee, my best friend and the banker's son. He came to school with a swollen lip. Although a boy that age having a swollen lip may not be extraordinary in itself, the cause, as he explained it, certainly was.

Greg's dental braces got stuck the night before as they did sometimes. Whenever that happened Mr. McNamee, an honest human being and a gentle father, used to take him to the orthodontist in Atkinson. But this time Greg's father insisted that he would have to try to fix them himself because he had suddenly realized, he said, it was costing him "an arm and a leg" with the orthodontist. Therefore, the banker-father declared, he was going to do it himself, saying to his uncertain and somewhat nervous son that he had observed the doctor often enough to do the job himself. "Nothing to it," he assured his son. As he was trying to fix the braces over his son's pleas, however, his pliers slipped and hit Greg hard in the mouth, although the problem was eventually solved in the process. The poor boy said his mouth bled almost all night and his swollen lips proved his ordeal.

Surrounded by his friends, Greg said forlornly, "he never tried anything like that before." "But, why?" the boys inquired in unison.

"He said my dental braces were costing him a fortune," Greg said unhappily, repeating his father's comments and feeling his dental braces as if they were the cause of his unhappiness. "He just got the bill from the orthodontist in Atkinson who fixed my teeth, and got very upset and said that he couldn't afford it any more."

"Yeah, but he owns the bank, doesn't he?" one of the boys said. "It's all his money."

"My dad says he isn't making enough money from his bank business," Greg said in defense of his father. "Anyway, maybe I should've been born with straighter teeth."

The boys were dismayed more because of the reasons for what happened than at the actual event. Parents complaining about the cost of child-rearing had been virtually unheard of in Laurinville, especially from someone who owned the bank. We returned to our playing but Greg's sudden misfortune seemed to linger on.

Later I took Greg aside.

"Greg, do you know if your father has been going to those Green Palm Seminars?"

Greg gave it a thought, then nodded and said, "I think so." He had also seen the glossy introduction to wealth and fortune with happy faces on the cover.

Then I asked what I considered a very important question: "Greg, have you looked at you dad's palms lately?"

The banker's son thought for a while and shook his head, apologizing for his lack of keener observation. Greg was not the observant kind anyway.

"When you get home today," I told him, "look at his palms and see if they are green. Call me about it later."

Greg had no idea what I was talking about but promised he would do that. I told him that, as best as I could guess, it was some sort of disease that was spreading. For all I knew, it could really be a disease.

Event number two was Mrs. Wilson. On that day she wore gloves even though the day was fairly warm. She announced, to a chorus of sympathy from us, that she had contracted poison ivy while working in her garden. Some boys and girls offered to bring ointments and solutions for her affliction. The class was abuzz for a while with the recounting of everyone's experience with poison ivy. But her lecture on the American Founding Fathers that followed struck me as somewhat odd. Describing the founding philosophy of America, her personal favorite and repeated subject, she never once mentioned liberty and justice related to the founders of the nation, which she had never neglected to mention before. Instead, with this lecture she described the Founding Fathers as believers of "wealth and fortune for everybody in America." Stranger still was the way her lecture seemed to recite the Green Palmer manual word for word. She ended her lecture by saying that it was this philosophy of wealth and fortune for everybody who pursued it that "made America the great nation it is today."

Most of my classmates didn't seem to notice anything different about our teacher, but I noticed that Mrs. Wilson had also been losing some of her usual crisp appearances. Her normally meticulous personal grooming had turned somewhat careless of late, almost like a person who had just discovered that there was more to life than good grooming. Now she looked lackadaisical with herself and meandering with her class, eyeing the clock frequently as if she was anxious to see her day end. On the account of the poison ivy, she continued to wear her gloves for the next few days. Every day containers of ointments and solutions were placed on her desk by some of our worried classmates.

Event number three had to do with my father. On the following Sunday we had invited Miss Casey to have dinner with us at our favorite restaurant, where Father and I often had our Sunday dinner out. The owner of the restaurant bought his pastries from my father's bakery which, he said, were partly responsible for his good business. We had our special table and enjoyed our dinner. Father was in good humor and entertained Miss Casey graciously.

The odd thing happened when we were standing by the cashier while Father was paying the bill. When he pulled out his money to pay, I was very certain that I saw the marked twenty-dollar bill among the money with which he paid the bill. The folding and ink smudges were unmistakable. It was the money that should have been turned in at Mr. Rogers' office as Father had promised. I was about to holler at the discovery, but caught myself in the nick of time. The words stuck in my throat because I remembered that Father had told me the very next day that Mr. Rogers, the police chief, was very pleased with my good deed and that he would do his best to find the owner. Was it possible that he gave the chief a different twenty, one of his own? Or was my father lying to me? I could ask about it at the police station myself but I was afraid of what I might find out.

What was also disquieting was the fact that my father complained about how expensive the dinner had been and how prices on everything were going up. He even speculated loudly about whether he should charged more for his pastries. Miss Casey and I exchanged glances behind Father's back as if we knew what was going on. But we actually didn't know what was going on with him or with anyone else in the whole town of Laurinville.

When Greg McNamee called me back that night he was almost hysterical. Not only was his father's palm green, Greg said, he had also seen many other people in town who had green palms! What's going on, Greg desperately wanted to know. He naturally associated green palms with giving children fat lips.

"Another thing," Greg whispered as if fearing someone might hear him, "my dad came back from a bankers' meeting in Atkinson today and brought a snapshot of himself with the other bankers who were also there, raising their wine glasses in a toast. You know what, Mikey? They all have green palms. I'm afraid Dad is going to try to fix my braces again."

I told him what I had seen in the glossy introduction to wealth and fortune, and also on my paper route, and suggested that the green palm seminars and some of the things happening in Laurinville might be connected. After some more discussion and exploration of these phenomena, we decided on two courses of action immediately. First, we should speak to Mrs. Wilson, still our best source of information at school, about it, and second, we should secretly observe one of the seminars to see what was going on there.

Greg and I agreed not to talk to anyone, at least for a while, about our discussion and decision. Things were strange all around us but they were also so exciting. We were afraid but, like typical boys, we felt adventurous too. Nothing like this had ever happened in our town before.

The next day Greg and I went to Mrs. Wilson's office during a recess. Her office door, which was usually open at all hours during the day, was closed and I knocked. After a moment of hesitation, she said, "come in."

I had been in her office many times before and was familiar with it. In fact, it was only last week that I had changed the flowers on her desk. When she commented that I was such a good flower arranger, I told her that I did that all the time for Mother. Of course, Mrs. Wilson knew all about our family visit to Mother's cemetery every week. Once I wrote an essay about the cemetery for her.

Greg and I stood there, somewhat uncertain of our mission and her reception.

"Well, boys," Mrs. Wilson regarded us with a slightly turned face. "What can I do for you?"

Somehow she made us feel we had interrupted her at an inopportune time. She must have been engaged in something terribly important because there was definite impatience in her voice and in her manner as she received us. The way she said, "What can I do for you?" seemed to suggest that, unlike her usual self, Mrs. Wilson was in no mood to do anything for us. It was like, "State your business and leave."

Greg hesitantly told her what happened to him. He described how his father hurt his mouth on the account of expensive dental braces and about the green palms he had seen on the bankers and some other people in town, some palms greener than others. Greg, impressed by Mrs. Wilson's less than welcoming reception, made a halting, poor narrator of his story. That only added to Mrs. Wilson's impatience.

I then told her about my father and his own green palms, and how the glossy brochure with pictures of happy men and women seemed to have affected him in very unhappy ways. Among other things, he was also forgetting to write me notes and refusing to do our weekly visits to Mother at the cemetery.

Mrs. Wilson listened to us with an obvious lack of attentiveness and none of the friendly interest which we always expected from her.

"Well, boys," she said when we had finished our stories, "I will tell you, there is nothing to worry about."

To our surprise, we were not getting her sympathy. She summarily dismissed our anxieties and perplexities! We were, to say the least, quite disappointed.

Reading our faces, she reached and pulled something out of a stack of booklets and paper on the corner of her desk. It was the same glossy introduction to wealth and fortune that my father had received from the Green Palm Seminars.

"Well, Michael," she said as she put the attractive looking manual down in front of us, "is this what you are talking about?"

"Yes, Mrs. Wilson, that's the one," I eagerly responded, pointing to it and almost jumping to grab it as if it were the culprit of all our anxieties and perplexities, and my personal woes and sorrows. "That's the one I am talking about."

"I have read it myself," our teacher said, ignoring my excitement as she tried to turn a few pages. But she was having some difficulty turning the pages because of the gloves she was still wearing. The poison ivy was still bothering her. "I even marked some pages myself that were good. Listen."

Mrs. Wilson then started to read a section from it:

"'Every affluent investor is in a position to benefit from our recommendations. They include broad investment strategies to increase yield and position for growth as well as immediate buy and sell tactics for today's markets,' etc., etc."

Our social studies teacher then went on with another:

"'We have attractive stocks with a happy combination of income and growth potential. In this era of falling interest rates, stocks with attractive dividends present an increasing appeal. And it's just that appeal which we believe provides a basis for appreciation as well as growth,' etc., etc."

Then with another:

"'It's always been difficult for individual investors to participate in investment opportunities involving privately-held companies—yet many privately-held or closely-held businesses present a potential for both income and/or growth. A new concept to allow investors to take part in selected private stocks is described in this manual,' etc., etc."

To me it was all foreign language. Even Greg, the banker's son, sat totally uncomprehending. Mrs. Wilson put the manual down and looked at us quizzically above her glasses. Her pale blue eyes seemed rather unfriendly.

"What's wrong with growth potential and stock accumulation?" she inquired. Then she added some more "What's wrong with"s, still using the very puzzling language.

Of course, we had no answer. Both Greg and I fumbled for words. Seeing that we were no match for her knowledge and her new language, she repeated a few more questions and quotations for good measure. She then said something about the "importance of business-oriented curricula" that she wanted to see "emphasized at our school." Our teacher laughed a hearty laugh, almost like a man who is exceptionally satisfied with himself. I was getting upset.

"But, Mrs. Wilson, it's the green palm," I pleaded with her. "It's the green palm that's making people change. You see, my father, and Greg's father, both of them—"

Before I could finish my words, Mrs. Wilson assumed the strangest face I had ever seen and took off one of her gloves.

"You mean like this?" she said as she held up her hand,

which had a light green palm, and waved it close to our faces.

I stopped breathing. For all I knew, so did Greg.

Repeating "you mean like this?" she took off the other glove. Mrs. Wilson held both of her hands up, green palms facing us just like the one I had seen on the billboard. I tried to turn away from them as if a terrible disease was about to touch me. Our teacher let out another manly laugh, this time throatier than before.

Greg was absolutely dumbfounded: "How about the poison ivy, Mrs. Wilson," he cried. "Is it all gone?"

Chapter Eight

On the way to school the next day I came upon Mrs. Yalta struggling with her groceries. Apparently she had bought more than she could comfortably carry.

Naturally I offered to carry a bag for her, for which she was grateful and gave me some cookies for my help, which I consumed immediately. But since her home was somewhat out of the way I found myself being slightly late to school. We were always encouraged to put service to the townspeople above all else, and my offer to help Mrs. Yalta seemed perfectly routine. It was a good deed, though it was such a natural response for a Laurinville boy that the thought of a good deed had not even occurred to me. It was expected of all children in our town.

Therefore I was surprised to face what I thought was a rather severe reprimand from Mrs. Wilson on that account. She had put her gloves back on. She said, in front of the whole class and even after I had offered my explanation, that she no longer tolerated tardiness in her class no matter what the cause. The teacher said, more surprising to me than anything, that Mrs. Yalta should have paid someone to help her with the load or should have bought only so much as she could carry by herself. When I ventured to say that Mrs. Yalta might not have had enough money to get help, the teacher was scornful: "Well, that's her problem," she said. "We can't help that."

We had never heard anything like this from any adult in

Laurinville, much less from our beloved Mrs. Wilson. I was upset and disheartened about the whole episode. I almost wanted to shout to her, "Is this what happens when you become a Green Palmer, Mrs. Wilson?"

After lunch, still unhappy with the turn of events and with the scolding I took in particular, I decided to go play with the boys. There is a large clearing in the back of the school, which used to be our favorite spot. A good number of pine trees were still standing to give the area a nice shade and a comfortable feeling of enclosure. The clearing extended several acres farther out and ended where the first strip of farmland began. The forest of pine trees continued eastward, and included the location of my mother's cemetery. The squirrel I had seen the other day was one of the many small animals that inhabited the woods. Usually after lunch we congregated there to play games, frequently throwing the pinecones at one another.

As I approached the area after lunch I saw some of my classmates huddling behind a large pine tree, laughing and nudging each other. They were so absorbed in their little fun that none of them even noticed my approach.

I leaned over them to see the object of the boys' avid attention. It was a sheaf of pages apparently cut out from a magazine. I held my breath: They were the pictures of almost naked women! Later I was told that the pictures were cut out from a swimsuit catalogue somewhere in the west which advertised and sold tiny swimsuits. The pictures showed beautiful young women in various poses who were practically naked. Their bodies were barely covered by the stringy see-through things they apparently called "newly-fashionable" swimsuits. The boys were obviously not interested in the swimsuits. None of us had ever seen anything like it in our whole lives.

"Where did you get these pictures?" embarrassed and ashamed, I asked no one in particular.

"From a man," said John Sabella, the smallest and the sweetest among our group and almost always sickly. His father, a farmer with thining hair at the top and a lot of energy, was also an enthusiastic coach for the boys' basketball and the girls' soccer teams. Whenever John got sick and couldn't deliver his paper, he almost always called on me to take care of his *Observer* route for him.

"What man?"

"A man with funny palms."

"Green palms?"

John nodded and said, "there is something else he gave me," pulling out a piece of paper from his pocket. "He wanted me to tell my friends and parents about it. I have a whole bunch more."

What the man with green palms had given John was a small advertising bill, announcing something called "Adult Store" to open soon in Laurinville. It promised to have all sorts of things and gadgets for "mature pleasure," showing beautiful women in skimpy clothes obviously enjoying mature pleasure. The bill also had more smiling faces of grown men and women who seemed extremely satisfied with themselves. Lately we were seeing a lot of smiling faces in Laurinville.

"Adult store?" we reacted in unison, uncomprehending. Stores were always simply stores where adults and children both bought things.

"Must have high shelves," one boy suggested, then turned to John to tease him: "Too bad, you're too short to go there."

We were also puzzled by "mature pleasure." One of the ideas that we seriously entertained was that it might be about knitting. But the pictures of women and men seemed to suggest something more enticing than knitting. Turning our attention to the awful objects we had in our hands, I suggested that we rip the sheets up, throw them in the trashcan, and tell nobody about the incident. Not all willingly agreed. Some boys dropped the shredded swimsuits into the trashcan with considerable reluctance. As a parting gesture, I recommended that in the future we never accept anything from any adult we didn't know.

"We should never accept anything from strangers or talk to strangers," I made them swear to it. However reluctantly, one by one they did. We returned to class after a halfhearted pinecone fight, both excited and exhausted from this experience which was entirely new to us.

Also new to Laurinville, the Wednesday *Observer* ran letters from some townspeople who were irate with Atkinson. A few letters accused Atkinson of draining too much water from the reservoir for largely wasteful things like gardening and car washing. Other letters darkly hinted at some action if Atkinson did not heed. One particular writer called the whole thing a "moral equivalent of war." I had no idea what that meant. One letter went so far as calling for the mayor's resignation. The letter insisted that Laurinville needed "new leadership" who would be more forceful with Atkinson on the water issue.

The bitter tone of some of the letters was astonishing by Laurinville standards of gentility and friendliness. Nothing like this had ever appeared in the history of the *Observer*, or of Laurinville, for that matter. What was more puzzling was that I overheard Mr. Willis, the newspaper's owner, a tall man who was as gentle in person as his newspaper, tell someone at the one-room office that the angry letters "should be good for increasing the *Observer*'s circulation." Increasing the circulation? I wondered, what for? I tried to see if his palms had turned green but his hands were all covered with printing ink, so I couldn't tell.

My visit to Miss Casey's auto repair shop, to talk to someone I could trust, also ended unhappily. It had to do with one of her customers, a Laurinville widow on a small pension, whose high-pitched voice could be heard from a block away. As she complained about the "shabby treatment" she was getting from the shop, she kept referring to herself as "customer king." She was upset because her car had not been repaired at the time she had expected it. Miss Casey was patiently trying to explain to her that for some reason the parts had not arrived and that she would volunteer to drive the widow wherever she needed to go. But the customer-king would have none of it. She kept demanding "immediate customer satisfaction." She wanted her own car repaired right away, at that instant.

"I am a customer," the normally modest widow declared. "And a customer is a king, isn't it? I demand to be treated like a king. I want my vehicle right now."

She repeated this declaration of her status as customer-king several times more. She even threatened a lawsuit, mentioning an Atkinson law office called "Thorson, Davies & Johnson," or something. She said they were "the nastiest and meanest lawyers in Atkinson" who would not stop at anything. Miss Casey finally succeeded in persuading her royal customer to calm down. The dissatisfied royalty finally left with a flourish.

"Boy, for a widow who lives on a small income she sure demands a lot," one of the mechanics said loudly, which caused a round of laugh at the shop. Miss Casey, unaffected by the guffaw of her colleagues, shook her head, worn out and forlorn as if reacting to both the royal customer and her own colleagues.

"I don't know what's gotten into people lately," she said. "I have never seen anything like it in all my life."

She wiped her hands clean before stroking my hair, perhaps more to calm herself down than anything. To my relief, her palms were not green. Miss Casey said customers now complained about everything. Even the slightest dissatisfaction caused their irritation. People were suddenly becoming very demanding and conscious of their rights as customers. Threats of lawsuits were now increasingly becoming commonplace.

"So what's new at school, Mikey?" she inquired.

I hesitated to add any more bad news, but nevertheless told her about the pictures of women in swimsuits and the "adult store" soon to open in Laurinville. The auto-mechanic smiled when I described the swimsuits but frowned when I mentioned the new store.

"What's an adult store?" I asked.

"Well," she was silent for a moment, trying to find the right way to explain it. "I guess it's a place where boys like you wouldn't find anything useful."

Then she added, as if to herself: "I guess sooner or later it had to come to Laurinville."

That odd remark reminded me of Mr. Yalta who had said something similar.

Miss Casey asked me about Father and I had to tell her about his increasingly forgetful and often alarmingly lazy behavior. He often forgot to bring home my doughnuts, and almost always forgot to write me notes any more. The last two Sundays he sent me to Mother's cemetery alone. "Living is for the living, not the dead," he had said something like that. Whatever its meaning might have been, I didn't like that kind of talk from him about Mother. I also told her that Father had asked me how much money I had in my college account at the bank. When I told him Father went into deep thought, occasionally muttering to himself, "capital growth," "easy stocks," "risk-free investment," or something like those from the Green Palmer manual.

"Did he ever ask you to give him your college fund?" Miss Casey asked.

I said he didn't. But I told her that I could tell from Father's expression that he would like to have my money. She told me to hide my bank book where Father couldn't find it. I promised to do what she told me. Then our discussion turned to the angry letters in the *Observer* accusing Atkinson.

"I don't know what's going on around here," she said. "But something strange is going on and I don't like it. The whole town seems to be going wild. Even your father is being affected by it."

She said she had an idea. She was going to call for a town picnic soon, made especially attractive by her famous bass fry, to see if things could be discussed more calmly about the water situation with Atkinson.

"These men might talk sense if they enjoyed some of my fish fry."

We talked happily about planning a big town picnic at the park. Then a thought occurred.

"Miss Casey," I asked what amounted to a foolish question, "why don't you join the Green Palmers like the others?"

The best auto-mechanic in Laurinville smiled that sweet smile and thought the matter over. Then she said simply, "I don't need wealth and fortune, I guess. I have everything I need."

Chapter Nine

I was busy the next few days helping Mr. Dixon and Jamie Yarborough.

Mr. Dixon owned the largest store in town, where Father and I bought our groceries and weekly flowers for Mother. I often helped him with small jobs. My job this time consisted of changing price tags on the groceries. (Mr. Dixon called it "marking it up.") The owner would figure out how much mark-up he wanted on the merchandise and I would change the price by pasting the new tag over the old one. The new price tag was accompanied by the word "SALE" stamped next to it. Since his store was the largest in Laurinville, Mr. Dixon said, he could afford to raise the prices and no one would notice the change.

He also told me to watch for the "shoplifters," a word he used to an unsettling effect.

"Shoplifters?" I had never heard the word before.

"They are the people who walk off with things without paying for them," the store-owner, who had until recently been gentle and honest, explained. "That's started happening lately."

"Why would anybody do that, Mr. Dixon?" I inquired because I had never heard anything like that taking place in our town.

"Well, people will steal you blind," he said, using what I considered a coarse expression. "You have to watch them all the time."

His comment reminded me of the customer-king at Miss Casey's repair shop. So I described what I had seen to Mr. Dixon. His reaction somewhat surprised me.

"Ha, customer-king!" the store-owner fairly shouted. "Customers are kings, all right, as long as they pay for their stuff. But if they don't pay, they are common thieves! It's their money that makes them kings. No money, no king! So, there!"

Then Mr. Dixon scanned his store quickly to make sure no one was around, although it was late and hardly anyone was in the store, and pointed to something in the corner close to the ceiling. It was placed where people couldn't see it easily. I looked more carefully and spotted a small machine with a lens on the tip of it. The machine slowly moved side to side like a sentinel guarding the whole store.

"That's a hidden camera," Mr. Dixon whispered. "I just got it installed yesterday. It takes pictures of everybody, including the shoplifters. So whenever it looks at you, smile."

The owner actually smiled as he said so. I had worked for Mr. Dixon before on many small chores. The store had been almost as familiar a place to me as my school and Mother's cemetery. But now something was different about it. The store was brightly decorated with many pictures of pretty women smiling, apparently satisfied with their shopping. There were also signs that guaranteed "consumer satisfaction" and that promised "service" as the "number one priority." Mr. Dixon's store was also equipped with pleasant-sounding music that played all day long although nobody seemed to notice that it was playing. When I told him that the store looked a lot prettier, the store-owner looked proud.

"Psychology, son," he said, smiling and pointing to his head. "You must use psychology to do good business."

Whatever it was, psychology had apparently changed the

people who came to the store. There used to be much noise with people talking to each other and children trying to make the best of the situation to play. But, now, they were mostly silent. The children were restricted to the shopping carts, properly seated according to the instruction, and were severely scolded by their parents for being playful. Often mothers pulled their little children by the arm in such a hurry that their short legs could not keep up with the adults. People used to take their time, greeting each other in the aisles and exchanging the latest on their families and relatives. Often Mr. Dixon himself, interrupting whatever he was doing, would chime in. Now, they mostly hurried in, bought what they needed, and left the store as if in a great hurry. Mr. Dixon now talked less but smiled more.

The store had become brighter and more soothing with the music and all. But the people seemed to have no time to notice or enjoy the changes. Even the poster with a pretty woman who says, "SHOPPING AT OUR STORE GIVES YOU A WARM FEELING," seemed to go unappreciated. Overall, the brighter the store became, the more somber its customers became.

Psychology must have been a good thing for Mr. Dixon, however. More than once after the store closed, he grinned at the day's sale and gave me an extra quarter for my part in it.

"Psychology is working," he would say to no one in particular. "Psychology is working."

When I asked him what this psychology was the store-owner gave me one of his grins.

"It costs money, Mikey," he said, pointing to his cashier's register. "It costs a lot of money to get it from the people who sell it."

It was during the few days that I worked for him that Mr. Dixon's palms were gradually turning green. I wondered if it was the Green Palmers who sold him the psychology.

Beginning at about the time I had grown up enough to no longer require Jamie's babysitting services, I was sometimes asked to help her with her work at the *Observer*. It was mostly cutting and pasting small announcements and advertisements to put in the newspaper. As the paper was small, so was its usual advertisement section.

But this time it was different. I hadn't been to her office for a while and was surprised at the changes. Jamie showed me the new machines that the newspaper had brought in just last week, which she was still trying to learn. She told me that it was all pictures now.

"You know, it used to be just little announcements and price advertisements?" Jamie reminded me. "It's all pictures now. Everything has to have a smiling woman in it. Sometimes just one big smiling face and barely anything else in it."

Her remark made me think about the Green Palm billboard on the day that I saw it for the first time. It was practically all picture also. My former babysitter called it an "attention getter." At any rate, Jamie's new machines were fun to work with. She could create any image she wanted on the screen and had it printed when she got what she wanted. She let me do some of her creative work, sometimes with funny results that made both of us laugh. Her work load had also multiplied since the last time I had helped her.

One of the layouts she worked on had the picture of a handsome young man with bright eyes, smiling sincerely, who was to be the "vice president in charge of public relations" at Mr. McNamee's bank. It was a new position, according to the advertisement, "created to better serve our customers."

When I wanted to know what public relations was Jamie said the strangest thing: "Oh, I guess that's being dishonest to people."

I didn't understand how a man so sincere looking could be in charge of being dishonest.

"Everybody nowadays seems to advertise," my former babysitter said in response to my puzzled look. "Advertise, advertise. Advertise anything. Mr. Willis wants me to attend a school for 'Marketing Techniques' to learn more about advertising."

She also told me that there were some people, possibly from Atkinson, who came to talk to Mr. Willis about increasing the circulation. They advised the newspaperman to make his paper more "yellow," a word Jamie did not understand. When she asked Mr. Willis about the meaning of the word, he merely smiled and winked at her.

"Yellow?" I tried to figure it out. "Could it be printing the paper with more yellow ink?"

Jamie said she thought it meant something different but didn't quite know. At any rate, she noted that the *Observer* had started running more "entertaining" stories and letters from people. We were talking about the angry letters from some readers over the water issue with Atkinson and the mayor's handling of the situation. Jamie told me that these changes in the paper had definitely increased its circulation.

"People are now more interested in reading the paper, for sure," she acknowledged.

The last piece we worked on together was the announcement for the upcoming town picnic. Jamie volunteered her opinion that the picnic would be an "interesting one."

Working for Mr. Dixon and Jamie made me miss the opportunity to go to one of the Green Palm seminars with Greg as we had planned. Instead, Greg had to go with John Sabella, who also reported having trouble with his father. Mr. Sabella, the enthusiastic coach of the boys' basketball and the girl's soccer, had started talking about the next season already. He was very upset, according to the young Sabella, that neither of his teams had recorded a winning season that year. "Winning is not everything," Mr. Sabella, who mostly hollered when he talked, was heard hollering to himself. "It is the only thing."

John told us that his father had read about a famous coach in a town called Green Bay and started talking like him more and more. As a result, he wanted to play only the best players on the team, rather than every boy and girl taking turns playing. That meant, John Sabella said, that he was not going to be on his father's team any more. John was unhappy that his father made fun of his small frame and sickly constitution. Mr. Sabella told his son many times that he "would amount to nothing, certainly not a very good basketball player."

John, the normally sweet and sensible boy, was in tears when he told us what was happening at home with his father. When asked, he wasn't quite sure about his father's palm color.

At any rate, they told me that they had had a great time watching the Green Palm seminar, looking through one of the windows. Greg and John described the seminar as a simple ceremony for the new members who "ate money" as part of their membership initiation.

There were three smartly-dressed men, in dark green suits with a Green Palm badge on their lapels, the boys reported, who administered the pledge. Standing up toward the large Green Palm banner, they pledged their allegiance to the Green Palm. As Greg remembered it, with John's help, it went like this:

> *I pledge my allegiance to The Green Palm, and to my wealth and my fortune for which it stands—mine and mine alone—may it bring me my wealth and my fortune in abundance.*

Then one of the Green Palmers made a speech about wealth and fortune. He repeated sayings like "Nothing succeeds like success," "A sucker is born every minute," "The survival of the fittest," in his speech. The boys reported that the speaker finished his "motivation-speech" to rousing applause from the audience.

"Ladies and gentlemen," the leading man said, as little John tried to mimic him to good effect, "now, the time has come for the highlight of the evening: The initiation ceremony for our new Green Palmers."

Greg and John were particularly impressed with the money-eating part of the seminar and described the scene in some detail.

The leading Green Palmer motioned his assistant, who brought him a small box. The leading man proceeded to open the box with an air of great ceremony. Reaching down, he brought out a small bundle.

"Money," he said, holding up the bundle so that everyone could see, "is the essence of the Green Palm Way of Life as well as the lifeblood of all that is holy and natural. Our sacrament and ritual will commence with these dollar bills."

All three Green Palmers then took some of the money and distributed it to the new members, one bill for each person. Each new member held the money with both hands with a great deal of reverence.

Satisfied that all the new members held a dollar bill each, the leading man again motioned his assistant, who pulled down a screen from the wall just below the Green Palm banner. The leading man then proceeded to turn all the lights off. The assistant walked to the back of the audience to operate a projector. Soon, the enlarged image of a dollar bill appeared on the screen. "The average dollar bill has a life expectancy of two years," the voice-over narrator said. "In that life span, the typical bill changes hands four-hundred and seventy-two times. Four-hundred and seventy-two times. (The screen showed the money changing hands from one person to the next.) In other words, the dollar bill goes through four-hundred and seventy-two different people, young and old, men and women, sick people and healthy people. (The screen then showed people sneezing, coughing, scratching, blowing noses.) On the money you are holding in your hands now is the collection of over one-thousand known pathological micro-organisms. All kinds of infectious fungi, ringworms, tuberculosis, salmonella, you name it (showing these germs magnified on the screen), pass from one person to the next—yes, on the money you are holding in your hands at this moment. The dollar bill is the filthiest single thing you will ever hold. It is home to virtually every germ known to mankind."

The image of all those germs magnified thousands of times lingered on the screen for a few more seconds for effect. Then the picture gradually faded and the lights came back on. One of the new members, a woman, who must have dropped her bill during the film showing, was looking around to find it. The leading Green Palmer found it near the woman, stepped on it with his foot and pivoted a full circle. He then picked it up and gave it to her. With trembling hands the woman received the money.

"The dollar bill you are holding in your hands," the leading Green Palmer said, "is perhaps among the oldest, most-widely circulated bills that we could collect specially for the ceremony. They are all five years old or older."

The assistant then started singing what amounted to a slow, almost religious song. (John did a credible job of imitating him.)

"Let us commence our initiation," the leading Green Palmer said above the singing. "Oh, All Mighty Green Palm, bless the new followers who are about to show their commitment to wealth, fortune, and the Green Palm Way."

The new members slowly turned the money the long ways and, moving it toward their mouths, started chewing the bill. A couple of people, including the woman who had earlier dropped hers, seemed to gag. But with the help and encouragement from the leading Green Palmer, they managed to eat the money without a further mishap. The assistant continued his singing until the last person had finished swallowing the sacrament.

("Why did they have to eat up the real money?" Greg, the banker's son, said, and we all laughed. "Why couldn't they use play money, instead?")

On cue from the leading Green Palmer, the new members, whose palms had just started turning green, arose from their seats. Holding their right hands up this time, they recited the Pledge of Allegiance in a rousing chorus:

> *I pledge my allegiance to The Green Palm, and to my wealth and my fortune for which it stands—mine and mine alone—may it bring me my wealth and my fortune in abundance.*

Their pledge, Greg and John remembered, rang throughout the auditorium in one joyous and purposeful accord.

Chapter Ten

Talk of war with Atkinson was now heard more frequently.

Several strong-minded readers wrote to the *Observer* saying that war was the only alternative. They had given Atkinson, one letter said, time enough to stop stealing water from the reservoir. Another letter argued that it was Laurinville's "moral duty" to teach a bad town like Atkinson a lesson so that the problem would be resolved once and for all. Rumors of war circulated freely and brave words were spoken by many.

The attack was soon diverted to the mayor of Atkinson. A cartoon in the *Observer* showed him as a giant, drinking from the small reservoir with a straw while a group of tiny, thirsty people—apparently from Laurinville—stood in line with empty buckets in their hands. The mayor had bushy eyebrows and a thick mustache, which made him look like a bad man.

One timid reader had written that he opposed the war because he didn't believe that blood should be spilt for water. In an irate response, a more patriotic reader said it was not just water that was involved. It was Laurinville's moral principle that was at stake. "No blood for water," the writer agreed, but if Atkinson's mayor were not taught a lesson now, he would continue to do that sort of thing to other surrounding towns. "He must be stopped now," the letter concluded. The hitherto gentle people of Laurinville were suddenly becoming excited about the prospect of a war with their neighbors.

In a similarly militant mood, more and more town flags appeared in stores and public buildings. For some reason people started tying green ribbons to the trees and gate-posts in support of war. The martial spirit was everywhere.

On a smaller scale, our school was becoming a war zone of sorts. Not only did the boys and girls no longer help Mr. Anderson with his housekeeping chores, they littered the school with abandon. Things were getting stolen (my sack lunch included) and there was talk of installing lockers for the school. The boys became rowdy among themselves and unruly in classrooms. The girls started putting colors on their faces in imitation of the smiling women in advertisements.

I often saw some of the boys together, away from the others, looking at something that amused them and laughing silly. I could guess what they were looking at in such delightful secrecy. I heard Mr. LaGrange, the principal, talking to one of the teachers about the "need for sex education." Some of the paper delivery boys talked about taking their money out of the bank to spend it in Atkinson. They said there was a game everyone was playing called "Super Hero Exterminators," in which the heroes kicked and chopped and bludgeoned anyone who came near their camp.

Speaking of games, the boys refused to spot the smaller ones among them some handicap points to make the outcomes fair. In playing kickball, our favorite game, for example, the big boys now insisted on having the same distance as the small ones for determining homeruns. As a result, the bigger boys always won, but, while they gloated with their one-sided wins, the games were no longer fun for the smaller boys.

Mr. LaGrange had other problems, too. The school was running out of money because the townspeople suddenly refused to pay to maintain their school. In desperation, he and

Mr. Anderson went away one day in an old truck and brought to school what they called vending machines. They were the size of a refrigerator which, to our amazement, dispensed sodas and candy bars at the push of a button.

"That should bring in some extra money for the school," Mr. LaGrange said to Mr. Anderson after they had installed the machines in two places where the students gathered most, "although we know they are bad for the students' attention span and health. But we cannot worry about that now."

One of the most shocking developments was the possible strike by teachers. We understood that, by going on strike, the teachers would simply refuse to teach unless they were paid more. Of the seven teachers, five had developed green palms. Mrs. Wilson was their ringleader, who persuaded the other two to join the rest for a strike.

"We must make this look right," I overheard Mrs. Wilson tell the other teachers in one of their strategy meetings. "Sure, this strike is for more money for us, not for anybody else. But we must tell everybody that it is for the students, it is for the students. Remember to say, it is for the students that we are going to strike."

Mrs. Wilson led the others in chanting in unison "It is for the students" at least eight times until everyone could say it in absolute sincerity. On my part, I had a tough time understanding what was meant by "strike." It was difficult for me to comprehend that teachers would refuse to teach in order to demand more money.

Mr. Miller, the much-pressured mayor of Laurinville, authorized Mr. Rogers to make himself a full-time chief of police and hire a deputy to help him. In announcing this action, the mayor said in the *Observer* that the streets were becoming dangerous places after dark especially for children. We were told to avoid being out on the street at night.

Already, the newspaper started a column called "Crime Report" which detailed the misdeeds of the wayward. Jamie, quoting Mr. Willis, told me that the Crime Report was quickly becoming a popular section of the paper. She had learned that it was that sort of news that made the newspaper more "yellow" and increased its circulation. In fact, according to Jamie, Mr. Willis had told his reporters at an editorial meeting to "look under every bed" to get stories, whatever that meant.

One day when I was getting ready to start my paper route, the man in charge of delivery motioned me into his office.

"Bad news, Mikey," he said, pointing to a stack of newspaper ready to be delivered. "John is sick again. Can you take care of his route?"

It was not the first time. I told him that I would handle his route as soon as I completed my own.

In the last few weeks, since the appearance of the Green Palmers, my paper delivery took less and less time to complete. There was less and less talk between the subscribers and the delivery boy. I simply put the paper in a box that had recently been erected by the *Observer*. Streets were becoming quiet and deserted. People were all staying inside. I could sense their presence, peering through the windows, many of them now with bars. Mr. Yalta still waved from the inside and Mrs. Yalta once in a while remembered to give me cookies. Mr. Shepeck's guard dog had learned to be a good guard dog. He growled ferociously whenever I came near him.

After my own route was completed, I went back to the newspaper office and picked up John's. His load was small. I thought I could finish it in no time. Since I had done this many times before, I had no trouble with his route. I hardly needed to look at the list of subscribers.

One of the last places on the list was Mr. Miller's. He lived almost at the edge of Laurinville, not far from his office as mayor. Often he took care of town business, such as it was, at his home. But as I deposited the paper in its place and turned around to leave, I spotted a small van parked in the corner of Mr. Miller's driveway. It was growing dark and the van was partially hidden behind tall hedges. I would not have noticed the van, except for the Green Palm logo on a white background painted on the side facing me. I assumed there was another one like that on the other side. The white in the logo stood out clearly even in the early evening darkness.

Then I heard laughter from what I guessed was Mr. Miller's living room. The breeze was pleasant, and the open window faced the small yard where I was standing. All I needed to do to see them was take a step or two to my right. I was wondering if the van belonged to those Green Palmers who had administered the money-eating ceremony that Greg and John had seen. There were only a few more houses left on my route, and I decided to take a look at the Green Palmers for the first time. My curiosity was simply too much.

There were two Green Palmers, sitting in the living room facing the mayor. I could tell they were Green Palmers simply because they wore a green suit and had a Green Palm badge on their lapels, exactly as Greg and John had described them.

"Mr. Mayor," one of the Green Palmers was saying ("Mr. Mayor?" I had never heard him addressed that way), "what you need is a 'tracking poll' to know exactly what people in Laurinville are thinking so that you can give them what they want."

The man described the thing called "tracking poll" for the mayor. He said it was composed of a "small group of people" "selected randomly" to "represent" the "cross-section" of Laurinville. By constantly "interviewing these people," the man said, the mayor could tell exactly what people were thinking and demanding at "any given time."

"So that," the man concluded, "you can maximize your leverage in controlling public opinion in anticipation of the shift in popular moods and trends, both for you and against you."

Whatever the meaning of what the man was saying, it seemed to have an impact on Mr. Miller who leaned over and listened carefully. Then the other Green Palmer, addressed as "Dr. Robert Lamb, the Scientific Psychologist," bespectacled and looking awfully knowledgeable, opened his briefcase at his side and pulled out long folded sheets of paper.

"Here is our data on computer printouts," the man said as he unfolded the sheets on the table in front of him so that the mayor could see them better. "The anticipated moods and trends for Laurinville indicate that you would be best served if you declared war on Atkinson."

Mr. Miller looked up and, frowning, said nothing for a while. I could tell that he was thinking hard.

"I know there have been some people who are opposed to blood for water," the Scientific Psychologist continued. "But you have been under pressure for some time to do something about a lot of things in this town that are not going very well."

"Heaven knows, there are—," the mayor tried to speak.

"They are not your problems to solve anyway," the first Green Palmer cut him short, as if the mayor's own thought was irrelevant to their discussion.

"War is always the quickest way to rally people behind you," Dr. Robert Lamb, the Scientific Psychologist, offered. "You know, rally around the commander-in-chief."

The words "commander-in-chief" seemed to have an electrifying effect on the mayor. He straightened himself, chest puffed up a little and chin jutting forward in the manner of a truly forceful leader.

"Think about it, Mr. Mayor," the bespectacled scientist told him. "If you can win the war quickly, who knows, you can even run for governor. Think about the victory parades, speeches, flag-waving—."

"Or the newspaper account of your leadership," the first man said. "'Under the brilliant leadership of Mr. Robin Miller, our town's new hero, the Laurinville Volunteers decisively defeated, etcetera, etcetera."

"You know we have a town picnic coming up soon," the mayor said after some thought, "I can perhaps hint at declaring war on Atkinson and see how they react."

"They will react positively," said Dr. Lamb, "I have no doubt about it. When things don't go well, war tends to become more attractive to a lot of people. You know what a famous French general said: 'There are few things in life that a nice war cannot fix.' We know it, too, because it is our business to know what attracts people. If you want to be popular and avoid criticism, Mr. Mayor, you must give people what they want."

I had never experienced war in my life and their war talk did not interest me that much. Slightly disappointed that they did not start eating more dollar bills, which was what I had really wanted to see them do, I was getting ready to leave. That's when I heard the word "tele-mind" mentioned, which almost made me jump with surprise. The first Green Palmer was telling the mayor that what Laurinville now needed was one tele-mind set in every household. One tele-mind set in every household!

"Once people are hooked on tele-mind," the man said, "all your problems are practically over, Mr. Mayor. You can manipulate their opinions and people won't have time to complain about anything. Nobody can stand up to the power of fifty-channel tele-mind offered around the clock."

Virtually every child in Laurinville had grown up knowing about tele-mind, although none had ever seen it. School book after school book explained the awesome power of tele-mind. From the pictures we had seen, the "set" was shaped like a box in various sizes. People normally sat in front of the set to "watch" it. The set beamed lights, some in color and some in black-and-white, into their heads, which came to them as pictures.

The person who watched it all the time, we were told, was called a "tele-minder." In Laurinville, tele-minder was usually considered the worst name one could call somebody. At school, likewise, the most severe penalty was assessed on the boys and girls who called somebody a tele-minder. It was considered positively the most uncivil offense in Laurinville's understanding of manners.

It was not surprising in light of what we knew of the machine. We had long since learned that the picture machine sucked the brain out of the tele-minder until he became practically as empty-headed and pliable as a zombie. The typical tele-minder would sit in front of the box day and night, totally lost to the world around him, acting and thinking according to the messages he received from the box.

"Unless you had no brains left," Mrs. Wilson used to tell us about it, "why would you sit in front of something like that for hours and days?"

Her descriptions of this infamous tele-mind machine had made us all shudder in great fear. Following a lecture on the machine by Mrs. Wilson, a few boys and girls had nightmares about it. Some of them reported that their nightmares consisted of being tied to a chair in front of the set or being condemned to watch it forever. Others described theirs in which their whole body was sucked into the box from which they could never escape.

   Professors of great learning said time and again, we were told, that tele-mind made people stupid, mistreat children, and do bad things to each other. It also made people talk funny—called "tele-mind talk," which consisted of simple childish babbling. To make matters worse, the typical tele-minder was equipped with something called a "zapper." With it he changed pictures constantly and restlessly, almost like a spoiled king who was always unhappy with himself, looking for something more exciting every minute. But, once hooked, the tele-minder could not turn it off. The beams that got into his head made him obedient to the tele-mind. Merchants, politicians, and even preachers used the machine to their advantage, by making people think stupid thoughts and do foolish things so that they could take advantage of them.

   Sometimes, out of adults' sight, children in Laurinville played a "tele-mind game" in which the loser was required to sit in front of a make-believe tele-mind set. The penalty consisted of looking as stupid as possible.

   Holy Toledo! It was *this* machine that the Green Palmers were suggesting to our mayor as a good thing for Laurinville!

   I was so shocked that I did not even remember the mayor's response to that suggestion. Like a real tele-minder, I delivered the rest of the paper in a completely blanked-out state of mind.

Chapter Eleven

Father finally said the thing that I had been dreading the most. He wanted my college money so that he could "invest" it in something that would give us many times more in return.

"This cannot fail," he said when I remained obstinate to his overture. "The opportunity is so good that I need everything I've got to throw in it. The man said this is the best he has ever had." Father then went on about something called "venture capital" which returned many times the investment. It was a "guaranteed profit." He also showed me, for good measure, another glossy brochure which contained more of the happy men and women who had apparently made a lot of wealth and fortune that way. Their testimonials seemed to have greatly encouraged my father.

Remembering what Miss Casey had told me, I stood fast and said no. Father had simply not been himself since the Green Palmers came to Laurinville, Miss Casey had said, and I should not go along with his ideas for easy wealth and quick fortune. She warned me of a possible new trick that psychologists invented called "behavior modification," "head game," and "guilt trip." Whatever these things were, they sounded positively evil to me.

Eventually my father ran out of patience trying to persuade me. He got upset with his obstinate son, hollering and, for the first time in my whole life, almost threatening with physical violence.

"Do you know how hard I work every day for you?" he

shouted after me as I left him and went to my room upstairs. "I am sick of working like a dog and being appreciated by nobody, not even by my own son." Then as if to himself, "why wouldn't he agree to make a lot of easy money with his little investment, uh, why? You can't fail with this one. You can't."

Exhausted from the struggle with Father, I threw myself on the bed, burying my face in the pillow. Then I heard a thud on the floor next to the bed. I raised my head to find that it was the present from Mr. Yalta which had fallen off the wall where it had been hung. Apparently shaken from my weight when I flung myself on the bed, it had dropped to the floor. I was too tired to hang it up again. I merely picked it up and stood it up, against the wall where it had fallen so that at least I wouldn't step on it by accident. The words "Liberty and Justice for All" gave me no comforting thought this time.

Father's hollering about his ungrateful son continued for a while. Then, I heard the door open and close and all was quiet. Apparently Father left the house. I tried to think hard but could not. All was chaotic and tiresome. All was simply too much for me to comprehend. Exhausted, I soon fell asleep.

The door opening and closing woke me up. I didn't know how long I had been sleeping. The pillow was partially wet from my hard sleep. There was some shuffling sound from downstairs but no voice.

Then I heard laughter, apparently a woman's, that I could not recognize. Father's mumbling voice followed. Both of them started laughing again as if something was terribly funny. I decided to get up and go see what was going on. Ever since Mother's death five years ago no woman's voice, much less a laughing one, had ever been heard in our house at night.

They were in the kitchen, a woman and Father. The woman, dressed in tight clothes showing her skinny body as if she did not eat well and with hair that was blown up high on her head, was sitting on Father's lap. There was much coloring on her face in the fashion of the swimsuit women. When she saw me standing on the stairs her laughing quickly stopped. Then she got up from Father's lap and sat on the chair on the other side of the table. My father was holding a bottle in his hand and taking a drink from it. Both of them looked as if they had slept with their clothes on and had not had time to shower or comb their hair. The air in the kitchen had a foul reek.

"Son, meet Miss Diane Maxwell, she is from Atkinson," Father waved his bottle and managed to point to the woman. His speech was slow and his breathing hard. Then to her he said, "Miss Maxwell, this is my son, Mikey."

She smiled sweetly and said: "Nice to make your acquaintance, Mikey, I heard about you."

I said, "Nice to meet you, Miss Maxwell."

Father and Miss Maxwell looked at me as if they expected me to go back upstairs. But I did not move. Miss Maxwell might be a nice person, but I did not like the way she looked and the fact that she had been sitting on my father's lap. Miss Casey, I was thinking, would never do that sort of thing. The thought of Miss Casey made me angry at Father and the woman. Although I understood little in the way of grownups, I felt sad for Miss Casey that Father was with another woman, especially one from Atkinson with tight clothes and terrible hair.

"Go on upstairs, son," Father said when I refused to move. "Miss Maxwell and I have some business to discuss."

"What business?" I blurted out, practically in tears. "How about Miss Casey? How about Miss Casey? Don't you think she is going to be upset about this? And she was planning a nice fish fry for us!"

The air seemed to freeze in that instant. Father and Miss

Maxwell suddenly straightened up. Awkward silence filled the house for a few seconds. My father stood up slowly and threw the bottle into the trashcan.

"Miss Maxwell," he said somewhat formally, "I'd better take you home."

Miss Maxwell smiled again, but like a woman who had just been told that the crowd had left without her, looking up at Father and me alternately. She slowly and thoughtfully got up from her chair and walked toward the door with Father. Then she stopped, turned around, and walked toward me. She stood there at the bottom of the stairs, her face on the same level as mine.

"Mikey," she said as she extended her hand, which was not green, "you are a wonderful boy. Your father should be so proud of you."

"Thank you," I said, extending my own hand to shake hers. "You are kind."

She patted my hand several times with her free hand, and turned around and walked out. I thought I saw tears in Miss Maxwell's eyes, which made me feel sorry for her and mad at my father. I had no idea what made him forget Miss Casey and rendered his appearance so shameful. Out of curiosity, I retrieved the bottle from the trashcan and put my nose to it. What was left in the bottle was the foulest stuff that I had ever smelled. The toxic odor from the bottle almost took my breath away. I couldn't understand how people could drink that stuff. There was always lemonade to drink when one was thirsty.

Back in my room, thinking about Miss Casey, Father, and the affecting Miss Maxwell, and everything else going on in Laurinville, I soon fell into an uneasy sleep and a series of strange dreams.

The town picnic was held on Sunday at the park. As expected, people flocked to Miss Casey's fish fry before they tried anything else that other people had brought. Father was seen helping her with particular attentiveness as if to make up for his misdeed the other night. He had a nice cook's apron on and told jokes.

It was there, however, that Greg told me something awful about John Sabella.

"John ran away from home," Greg whispered to me.

As the banker's son told me, John had come to him the same afternoon I did his route for him, and told him that he was going to run away.

"But, why?" I cried. It seemed I was raising the same question a lot lately.

As John told Greg, his father had become extremely critical of his chances to become a great athlete. Mr. Sabella, who was always running and exercising, often leading the townspeople on short marathons, had been reading many books on sports heroes who were wealthy and famous. John told Greg that his father talked about nothing but sports statistics and the great money the famous athletes were making.

"Do you know Mitchell Jordan is making five thousand dollars a basket? Do you know the average salary of major league players is one million dollars?" he would badger John anytime of the day. This reference to fabulous athletes was always followed by the unhappy realization that John Sabella was no budding Mitchell Jordan. People in Laurinville had never heard of Mitchell Jordan or those other wealthy players who were paid to play. (To my shock, Greg said Mr. Sabella wanted the town's name changed to Jordanville in honor of the man who got rich by playing.)

"Only people who *work* should get paid, not the people who

play," had been the general consensus that was always taught to the children in our town.

But to Mr. Sabella who, like many other townspeople, was suddenly developing an interest in different things, John's sickly constitution had apparently become a severe blow to his athletic dreams of wealth and fame. And he let his young son know about it.

"So he decided to run away," Greg concluded. He didn't know where the runaway had gone; Atkinson, which was also the nearest town, was his guess. As an aside, Greg said he had given him all his money from his piggy bank.

Running away from home was almost unheard of in Laurinville. The only, certainly the most famous, case in the town's living memory, was Mr. and Mrs. Blake who had eloped to get married when they were young. In spite of this history, the Blakes returned to Laurinville and lived, especially for the heroic late Mr. Blake, exemplary lives. That was a long time ago.

Greg said he heard from the grownups that Mr. Rogers and his deputy contacted the Atkinson police department about a runaway boy presumably in their town. The news was not good for Mr. Rogers, and Mr. Sabella, because there were so many other missing children that the Atkinson police had to search for.

The grownups in Laurinville, however, had other more urgent business on their minds. Under Mayor Miller's civic guidance, and Mr. Willis cheering on, and to the dismay of Miss Casey who had hoped for a more peaceful frame of mind to result from her fish fry, the talk at the picnic turned quickly to the possible war of the reservoir.

"All the townspeople in Laurinville know," Mr. Miller said to the crowd that had gathered around him, "that I have been rinsing my mouth only twice when I brush my teeth."

The crowd chanted, "we do, we do."

The mayor continued: "We've been making a lot of sacrifice in this town so that we can avoid a confrontation with our neighbors. But have we been getting any cooperation, any sacrifice from them? Nooooo. From the latest intelligence I have, they still wash their cars and water their flower gardens, if you can believe it."

The crowd was wildly enthusiastic about the direction of the mayor's speech. Instead of feeling peaceful and happy, the festiveness of the picnic made them feel courageous and daring about marching to a war.

"It's time for action, now!" the part-time mayor cried and the crowd roared its approval. The crowd cheered some more and shouts rose to a new height.

"But Mr. Miller, Mr. Miller," someone in the crowd yelled and waved his hand to be recognized. When they turned to find who it was, they saw Mr. Yalta. Groans were heard in the crowd.

"Yes, comrade Yalta," said the mayor with a slight smile. It was obviously intended to be poking fun at Mr. Yalta.

"Mr. Miller, and the good people of Laurinville," said the watch repairman from Russia, looking around, "let's not rush to war with Atkinson. There is still enough water left in the reservoir and we can peacefully share it with the people in Atkinson. No reason to rush to war."

"He is a Conservative!" someone said. Then murmurs of "Conservative" were heard making rounds in the crowd. From the snickerings that followed, I assumed they meant something bad about Mr. Yalta being a Conservative, whatever it was.

"Besides," Mr. Yalta said, trying to be heard above the crowd noise, "we now have so many problems in our town, and while we are exhausting ourselves for the war the problems are only going to get worse. War solves nothing. I know. I have been in two wars."

"Thank you, comrade Yalta," said the mayor mocking Mr. Yalta again. "But you are wrong about war. It does solve problems sometimes."

The last part of his comment brought the house down and drowned the feeble protest that Mr. Yalta was still trying to register. The mayor's comment reminded me of the two Green Palmers who had advised him on the merits of war in a troubled town.

"Action, action, we need action," several people shouted all at the same time. "We need action!"

"War, war!" others cried.

Who were these people who were crying out for war? I wondered. Could they have possibly been some of the Laurinville townspeople that I have known all my life?

Mr. Miller smiled and said in a dramatic voice: "As your commander-in-chief, this is my decision." He paused for effect: "We are giving Atkinson five days for our ultimatum. If they refuse to accept our terms by then we have no other choice, but to declare war. It is our moral responsibility to our children."

"What are our terms?" Mr. Willis inquired, his newspaperman's pen poised on his notebook.

Mr. Miller read from a written document a set of conditions in Laurinville's ultimatum for Atkinson. The conditions included, among other things, the reduction of water usage to ten percent, money compensation for Laurinville's inconvenience, and a promise never to make Laurinville suffer on account of drought, etc., etc.

The crowd again roared its approval. Somehow flags and green ribbons made their appearances, and many in the crowd waved the flags and tied the ribbons around their arms.

"In the meantime," the mayor shouted, "we must collect all the weapons we have and train in the proper use of these weapons. Anything that can be used to defeat the enemy will be collected."

Then the commander-in-chief appointed Mr. Anderson, the World War II veteran who hadn't seen battle in many decades, Laurinville's new Battle Commander and Weapons Sergeant. He would also consult the mayor on war strategy and drill the volunteers.

People wasted no time lining up in front of Mr. Anderson who made the list of weapons in Laurinville's possession. Mostly they were hunting guns, vintage rifles, BB guns, and other assortments of household items. Father listed the rifle which his own grandfather used in World War I. Mr. Shepeck volunteered his doberman as a scout.

Mr. Yalta, Miss Casey, Greg and I stood in the corner watching the scene of men ready to march to war.

"War doesn't solve anything," Mr. Yalta said.

"No blood for water," Miss Casey said.

"I am a good sling-shot," Greg said.

Then I thought I saw a man in what appeared to be a green suit just outside the picnic ground, leaning against a pine tree, as if amused by the whole spectacle.

"Look at that man!" I cried.

By the time I got their attention and looked again, he was gone.

"What is it, Mikey?" they inquired in unison.

"I thought I saw a man," I said. "He is gone."

Perhaps it was my imagination.

"What man?"

"A Green Palmer," I said, but without certainty. "He was watching us the whole time."

Chapter Twelve

The town of Atkinson did not take Laurinville's ultimatum kindly. Its mayor accused Laurinville of misdeeds concerning water and proceeded to issue its own ultimatum, similar to Laurinville's.

Mr. Anderson began organized drills for the "Laurinville Volunteers," as they were called. The drill generally took place at the park where the picnic was held. The men who were not at work came and participated. They lined up in three columns and, as Mr. Anderson barked the cadence, marched up and down the field. Many came dressed in what they considered the closest thing to being a solder's uniform. Most of them wore hats of one kind or another.

For the boys and girls in Laurinville, it was the biggest spectacle since the tornado. As soon as school was out, we rushed over to the park and sat on the grass and watched the grownups messing up steps and trying to figure out the difference between "about face" and "rear march" or between "column right march" and "right flank march." Mostly the drills were hopeless but they greatly entertained us. Some of us got sticks and, pretending they were rifles, marched alongside the volunteers, often doing better than the real soldiers.

The new battle commander wore his war uniform, now slightly too large for him, but he seemed to have regained some of his lost youth. He sharply reprimanded the wayward and, with great authority, demonstrated the proper drill technique. Sometimes the commander-in-chief himself, now decorated with a green ribbon tied diagonally across his chest, came out with words of encouragement and watched his army in training. According to the *Observer*, which detailed our training progress, the Atkinson townspeople were also engaged in a similar war preparation. This report did not surprise the Laurinville Volunteers.

Mr. Miller, in the meantime, organized what he called a War Council, made up of some important people in town. Father couldn't get on it because he worked mostly during evenings. The council membership called for free evenings for strategy sessions. The mayor and council met frequently in secret to hear the reports on their Volunteers' progress and map out their next move. This war preparation was so exciting and exhausting that Laurinville could not think of anything else. The lack of news about John's whereabouts was received with something less than urgency. War overshadowed everything. What the Green Palmers had predicted for the mayor was all coming true.

On the third day of war preparation, a most distressing event was reported in the *Observer*. The Atkinson mayor offered one thousand dollars to anyone who would come to him with information on Laurinville's strategy. From what we heard at the parade ground the next day, virtually all the Laurinville War Council members had called the mayor of Atkinson to offer the information. Stunned and furious, Mr. Miller counter-offered a two thousand dollar reward for information from the enemy. No sooner had he announced his reward than his office telephone started ringing. Not unlike Laurinville, Atkinson had its own people willing to sell information to the enemy. The mayor of Atkinson responded by raising the reward to three thousand dollars. Laurinville reacted with four thousand dollars. Atkinson raised it to five thousand dollars.

Well, Mr. Miller had no money to offer any higher. Laurinville could not continue the bidding war.

"These tawdry little people," the disappointed mayor declared, "they will do anything for money." He concluded, however, that, although the enemy might be better informed, Laurinville was superior in the patriotism of its citizens and the skills of its fighting men that Battle Commander Anderson was training so well.

Five days passed. Six days passed. Seven days passed. But Atkinson was unrepentant. It refused to yield to Laurinville's demand. Both sides knew pretty much everything about each other's war strategy, thanks to those "tawdry people," and were equally prepared for it. The stalemate was getting weary on both sides. I could tell that the soldiers, tired from Commander Anderson's endless drills, were anxious to get into action.

"We are anxious for action," one volunteer told the *Observer*. "We have been training for a whole week now. The troops can't wait any more."

Battle Commander Anderson also told the newspaper that he had informed the commander-in-chief that the troops were battle-ready. The mayor knew that he could not hold the present stalemate indefinitely. He had to move. People were getting impatient. So he made a decision for action, without informing anyone, since there was still the huge reward on strategic information.

This part of the War of the Reservoir is well-known history. Laurinville's town historian, Miriam Raynor, has preserved an extensive war record, with many personal accounts of war veterans themselves, in her library archives. There is little reason for me to go on in any great detail other than the part in which I participated personally.

The mayor's decision involved a surprise move from Laurinville to attack the Atkinson side of the reservoir and shut off its pipeline. This surprise move, if successful, would so stun Atkinson and demoralize its citizens when they turned on their showers in the morning that they would have to surrender. The mayor reasoned that nothing irritated people more than not getting the water when they stood under a shower head, ready for a good shower. Showing his deep understanding of human nature, the mayor guessed that the more ordinary the expectation (like a shower), the more irritated people got when it was not fulfilled as expected. History now considers that part of his psychology rather "astute" (which means "pretty good").

The commander-in-chief ordered Battle Commander Anderson to mobilize his troops at dawn for the attack. The mayor also asked some boys to act as supply troops, carrying food and drinking water in the event that the battle lasted until lunch time. Of course I volunteered, although I was one of the youngest, on the ground that I had marched with the soldiers at the parade ground many times and learned some of their military drills. My smart execution of "about face" and "rear march" convinced them that I was worthy of their trust. I was given a box of sandwiches to carry at the rear of the column, away from harm's way.

Now, some readers might try to guess, as many readers do when they read story books, that this might be the place where a twelve-year old boy named Michael Brown showed his heroism and saved his town singlehandedly. It would be nice to say that it was. But history cannot be altered. Unfortunately, my role in the War of the Reservoir was minimal. Besides, my heroism, if the reader will forgive me for calling it that, involved the *Green Palmers*, not the citizens of Atkinson.

The attack on the small contingent of Atkinson volunteers

guarding the reservoir was entirely successful. They were asleep, comfortable with the knowledge that they knew everything about Laurinville's strategy, thanks to the people who betrayed their town for money, and that there was no attack planned on the pipeline guardhouse. It was successful, but not easy. It would have been much easier had one of our soldiers, in his eagerness to fight, not started firing his rifle long before we circled around the reservoir to reach the other side. That gave the enemy troops plenty of time to get dressed and load their guns. After the first burst of gunfire from our volunteers, however, the enemy gave up. We saw their retreat in the distance, two of them still clutching their trousers and dragging their weapons, running madly in the general direction of Atkinson.

The Laurinville Volunteers were jubilant after an easy victory, which made them confident. So, instead of setting up outposts and sending out patrols, the soldiers started celebrating by eating breakfast. I was somewhat happy with the development because the sandwiches were getting too heavy to carry around. The distance between the town of Laurinville and the reservoir is little more than three miles. But, for a boy of my size, carrying sandwiches for at least thirty grownups over that distance was no easy task. The men ate their sandwiches and drank coffee for breakfast, while Battle Commander Anderson and several men were thinking of defending the guardhouse from a certain counterattack from Atkinson.

Commander Anderson's experience in World War II paid off in this early success. But not in the subsequent campaign. His knowledge was too outdated for modern warfare. He had forgotten about mobility, which was central to modern strategic thinking. He had figured that it would take at least two hours before Atkinson would send its main battle group and try to retake the guardhouse. By then the irate citizens without their morning showers would be fit to be tied. They might even overthrow their own mayor in revolt and the battle would have been won easily for Laurinville.

But Commander Anderson was totally wrong in this. The Atkinson army knew about mobility. They had their main battle group stationed only about one hour away from the reservoir just for such an eventuality. Thus, when the retreating soldiers from the guardhouse reached the main camp and reported what had happened, the Atkinson troops were ready to counterattack much sooner than anyone anticipated. (Since Mayor Miller had run out of money to equal the Atkinson reward for information, this piece of intelligence never reached the Laurinville high command.)

We were still eating our breakfast and enjoying our victory when the enemy counterattack appeared as a hail of gunfire. The reservoir was surrounded by miles and miles of open fields on all sides, and we could see the enemy, with his pennants waving and weapons held high, advance toward us. Puffs of smoke, and the sound a few moments later, indicated that they were firing at us. Battle Commander Anderson expertly timed the delay between the puff and the sound and told us that the enemy was about half a mile away.

"Hurry, get Battle Plan II," he cried. Two grownups rushed to the guardhouse to shut off the pipeline that carried water to Atkinson. Unfortunately, however, nobody had ever been inside the guardhouse before or studied how a modern reservoir operated. There were simply too many switches to pull and the men didn't know which ones controlled the Atkinson pipeline. The men scratched their heads, not knowing what to do. One of them rushed out to ask Commander Anderson what to do, but the World War Two hero knew nothing about reservoirs. The only thing he had ever done with the reservoir was fish in it a couple of times.

The enemy was now approaching rapidly. His pennants and weapons could be seen more clearly. They were menacing and I braced myself in fear and excitement. The sound now followed the puff rather closely. I could see, from the rear of our troops, the bobbing heads of the Atkinson soldiers through the overgrown weeds and bushes. Unlike the ragtag Laurinville Volunteers, the Atkinson troops seem to be wearing at least identical soldiers' hats, which made them look more menacing as they approached closer. They were now screaming something that sounded like "You Laurinville rats!" Our soldiers, hearing this, also fired their rifles angrily. However, neither side was apparently blessed with marksmen. Both sides missed their targets badly and could not hit anything.

Miss Miriam Raynor's history of the Battle of the Reservoir is more detailed in describing the hysterical few minutes in which the men desperately tried to figure out the correct switches to deny water to the enemy town. In the end, it was hopeless. As the enemy's approach was becoming dangerously close, Commander Anderson ordered the men to turn off *all* the switches in the guardhouse.

The main floodgates of most modern reservoirs are controlled by simple switches. What our volunteers didn't know was that one of the switches they pulled also controlled the main floodgate at the reservoir. What happened at the War of the Reservoir, as virtually all Laurinville townspeople know, is that there was no water left in the reservoir. The men simply opened the main floodgate and let all the water out. Not only did Atkinson get no showers, Laurinville also lost its water supply.

In the heat of the battle the decision had to be made and we cannot blame the brave men who risked their lives for their town for this minor mistake they made. Whether it would have been much better to allow both Atkinson *and* Laurinville to have a water supply by not turning anything off is an idle historical speculation. Of course, no one can tell, in retrospect, what course of action would have been better.

Our troops retreated safely, that is, to our side of the reservoir. I cannot say, as I observed this retreat personally, that it was orderly and dignified, for many of them dashed madly toward safety, jostling and elbowing each other in the process. They taunted the enemy from the safety of distance, once they reached the other side, before they decided to return to Laurinville. Fortunately, no one was injured or killed. The only mishap was that one of the men lost his wallet in the hasty retreat.

When Laurinville first heard the victorious news of taking the guardhouse, people were ecstatic. They said the war would be over in a matter of minutes when Atkinson had to go with no showers. The mayor was exuberant that the victory had been so easy. He made a speech at his office, which he called a "press release," about the great "heroes" of the battle and the welcome parade they would get. But when the town's water was shut off as the event unfolded, people weren't quite sure whether the troops were heroes or not. As the troops finally straggled in, most townspeople cheered but some jeered.

The soldiers did get their parade, history has so recorded, but nothing like the grand one they had expected. The turn-out was smaller and people, with their memories increasingly short by then, had all but forgotten about the battle. The more pressing issue was where the next shower was coming from.

Battle Commander Anderson went back at war's end to his job as our school's maintenance man, but this time to somewhat of a hero's welcome. Mr. LaGrange had a photograph taken of himself and the Commander of the War of the Reservoir in full gear and hung it in his office. Good thing, too, rain had finally come and filled the reservoir again by the time of the parade.

However, the mayor's approval rating soared. There was talk of making him Laurinville's "Mayor for Life." Those who disagreed, a small minority, said the mayor had spent too much of the town's money that could have been spent on other things. The war turned out to be a good thing for everyone. Well, not quite everyone.

"War doesn't solve anything," Mr. Yalta, one of those who disagreed, kept saying to anyone who would listen to him.

With the war over, things went back to normal in Laurinville, which by then meant that things went to the ways of the Green Palmers. The Green Palmers promised, in their special full-page advertisement in the *Observer*, an upcoming grand celebration for their 100th day in business in Laurinville. Everyone in town would be invited, the advertisement said. The gala event would also honor the heroes of the Victory at the War of the Reservoir.

It was going to be the greatest celebration, the Green Palmers declared, the town of Laurinville had ever seen.

Chapter Thirteen

Pressed for money, which the town had spent on the War of the Reservoir, Mr. Miller announced that the town of Laurinville was now going into "deficit financing."

A poll published in the *Observer* had indicated that the absolute majority (something like 93 percent) of the townspeople opposed paying higher taxes. To deficit finance, the town had to borrow money from other towns, including Atkinson. It was considered especially humiliating to have to borrow money from Laurinville's one-time enemy.

"But we have no other choice," the mayor told the *Observer*. "At least we don't have to raise taxes."

A critic asked the mayor who was going to pay for the borrowed money, saying "sooner or later, somebody has to pay."

The mayor defended his policy by saying that humiliation was much preferable to paying higher taxes. He further explained that he was assured by his "finance advisors" that the increased wealth and fortune of the next generation would take care of it. In the meantime, he told the townspeople, there was nothing to worry about.

"Don't worry," declared the popular leader of Laurinville. "Just say no to worries. Live today, worry tomorrow."

Whatever it was, deficit financing satisfied the townspeople who opposed virtually any kind of taxes. The "next generation" was too young to know about their own role in something called deficit financing. So no more critical voices were heard against the wartime commander-in-chief.

The school's financial problems, however, could not be solved this way. The condition went from bad to worse, as Mr. LaGrange often said. The principal ordered Mr. Anderson to get more of the vending machines installed at school, with a wider variety of candy bars and soda pops. (When Mr. Anderson died shortly after this installation some people whispered that having to move the heavy machines hastened his death.) Students were at first reluctant to drink soda pops and eat candy bars. But upon the encouragement of their principal and teachers who told them that to love the candy bars and soda pops was to love their school, they practically wore out the machines. Now the students called the places where the machines were installed their "hangouts." Boys and girls were forgetting to drink water when they were thirsty and to eat food when they were hungry. Many of them had to have a soda in their hands all the time and a candy bar to start the day. Some of them even ate candy bars for lunch. More school thefts were reported. The school needed lockers, the principal said. But to install lockers, a great deal of more money had to be made from the vending machines.

Students started arguing and fighting among themselves, even in the classroom. One boy was found to be carrying a knife, which prompted a talk of hiring a security guard. The boy said he had brought the knife to carve out his "girlfriend's" name on a pine tree in the back of the school. Some of us were shocked upon hearing the news. A girlfriend! The boy was only fourteen! No one in Laurinville ever talked about a girlfriend (or a boyfriend for that matter) until he was ready to get married. This incident also revived the urgent necessity for "sex education."

John Sabella was still missing. An article in the *Observer* said that his picture was put on milk cartons in Atkinson so that people might recognize him. But there were so many other missing boys and girls, the article said, that a new picture had to be put on milk cartons every week. All sorts of terrible stories circulated about what was happening to the missing children.

"This is terrible, this is terrible," Mr. Yalta would say as he scanned the *Observer* which now carried the "Crime Report" on its front page. When Mr. Dixon's store was broken into one night, it was on the front page. Mr. Rogers, the police chief, who, like his deputy, now carried his gun at all times, promised to arrest a suspect as soon as he could. Rumors of "outsiders" coming to Laurinville to do bad things made people lock up their houses more thoroughly. After dark hardly anyone dared to go out on the street. Boys and girls were told to look out for the "outsiders" and report to Mr. Rogers or his deputy any time we spotted them.

The vice president in charge of "public relations" at Mr. McNamee's bank arrived amid considerable fanfare and immediately got to work. When I went to the bank to make my deposits the man came out and shook hands with me. He looked me straight in the eye with a wonderful smile which showed his shiny straight teeth. His handshake was firm and friendly. He was dressed in a beautiful suit, such as was rarely seen in Laurinville. I was absolutely charmed by the young man.

"Hi, my name is James Toplin," he said. "But you can call me Jimmy. I am here to help you, to make you feel that you are part of our family. We want you to think that this bank is your bank, too."

I blushed with pleasure that someone was so helpful and sincere just for me. Mr. McNamee had never done anything like that before. The vice president in charge of public relations gave me a piece of paper, which he called a "survey" to fill out. There were questions like "What can we do to better serve you?" "Are you satisfied with our service?" "What are your most important financial needs?" "Do you approve the decor of our walls?" etc., etc. I filled it out as best as I could. The new vice president in charge of public relations was so dazzling that I didn't even remember the color of his palm.

My warm feelings were somewhat dashed when the handsome vice president rushed off, and said to the next customer who had just come in: "Hi, my name is James Toplin. But you can call me Jimmy. I am here to help you, to make you feel that you are part of our family. We want you to think that this bank is your bank, too."

Then the vice president proceeded to give him another of the surveys to do. Like Mr. Dixon's store, the interior of Mr. McNamee's bank had changed. Now bright colors and posters with smiling faces had replaced the traditional somber interior. A large sign that said, "OUR GOAL: WEALTH AND FORTUNE FOR OUR CUSTOMERS," was posted where everyone could see. The three comfortable chairs in the lobby, fairly worn with age and use, where people used to sit and chat had been removed. In its space stood a beautiful flower arrangement sitting on a marble-top table. It was only when I got closer to smell the flowers that I noticed they were artificial flowers. But they were more beautiful than any real flowers I had ever seen. Briefly, although I changed my mind immediately, I thought Father had a point in suggesting that we use artificial flowers for Mother.

The next two weeks or so, life was hectic everywhere in Laurinville. The Green Palmers had advised Mr. Miller (we have since learned from Miss Raynor's chronicle) to keep alive the memory of the war as long as possible. While the flags waved in air and the ribbons tied to trees, they advised him, no one was going to dare criticize him for the many social problems that plagued Laurinville.

So, like any good leader, the mayor followed their advice. He arranged all sorts of speeches and parades for every possible reason he could think of. Birthdays and funerals, even weddings, were used for speech-making and parades. On every occasion, Mr. Anderson was presented in his resplendent uniform as the Hero of the War of the Reservoir. After his death, his memory was kept alive in all possible ways. Mr. LaGrange, although unhappy that the parades were taking so much of his maintenance man's time away from his work, could not complain. Neither could other critics, notably Mr. Yalta, when everyone else was waving the flag and tying the ribbon. Anyone who was unenthusiastic about those speeches and parades was called a "Conservative," and people were afraid of being called Conservative. One letter writer in particular wrote to the *Observer,* saying people who were critical of the war should leave Laurinville and move to another town of their choice, implying Atkinson.

The speeches and parades were almost always followed by the announcement that they were "Sponsored by the Green Palmers, the Dream Makers," who had come to Laurinville to make it a "happy town." The announcement also reminded the crowd of the upcoming celebration, the greatest ever, to commemorate their first 100 days in Laurinville. Every occasion was greeted with a sign that said, "You Can Be a Green Palmer, Too."

At school, some of us were asked to volunteer our time to help the teachers to decorate the auditorium for the celebration. The war and the 100th day celebration had temporarily quieted the unhappy teachers who had been planning a strike. Now they were so involved in the parades and Green Palm preparations that they had almost forgotten about their unhappiness. Even Mrs. Wilson, their ringleader, seemed to have regained her energy.

"I feel very good about myself," I overheard her talking to another teacher. "I think life stands for the fullest self-actualization of one's potential earning powers. Accommodation of the realities is essential in the process and structure of economic empowerment."

She went on to say some more along a similar line. Of course, I had no idea what she was talking about. But the other teacher seemed to be profoundly affected by her colleague's philosophy. I say philosophy because, at that age, anything we didn't understand we simply called "philosophy."

On the days that I had no paper delivery I helped the teachers arrange seats, streamers, and posters. The sayings that Greg and John had heard in the earlier money-eating ritual like "Nothing succeeds like success," "A sucker is born every minute," "The survival of the fittest," and some new ones, appeared in signs and were posted on the walls. Mr. LaGrange said the Green Palmers were financing the preparations and we were to spare no expense. The principal hired some people temporarily, since the townspeople no longer volunteered their time to help, to clean up the school for the occasion.

They arranged the first two rows of seats for the "Charter Members," meaning those who had joined the Green Palmers before anyone else in town. Father was one of the charter members. He considered it a great honor and was excited about the special recognition to be given at the celebration. He got out his best Sunday suit and had it freshly pressed. One day he had put it on and was looking at himself in the mirror.

"How do I look?" he asked me, grinning and straightening

his tie and handkerchief in the breast pocket.

Father looked smashingly handsome, especially since he rarely dressed up like that. So I told him he looked good. He looked at himself this way and that some more, and carefully took the suit off and put it away in the closet.

My father had not badgered me any more about my college fund since the night he came home with Miss Maxwell. Now he made a special effort to make me feel better, patting me on the back and telling me that I was doing well at school, asking me about my "self-esteem" and "role models." Even the doughnuts reappeared, along with the notes. But there was something odd about all this. A twelve-year old may not know much in the way of the world, but he can tell if he is being truly loved by his father. Although he was complimentary about my schoolwork he had rarely asked to see my homework or reports. He would merely glance at them and say something like "a great job" without really meaning it. His notes alongside the doughnuts were much more beautifully composed than ever before. But they were not his own words. Father had never said things like "You are my sunshine, my only sunshine," or "Life is made of dreams, Go for it," and so on. When I showed these notes to Jamie, she laughed and said Father was quoting from something called "Whole-Mark Cards." She explained that people who were good with words were paid to write those pretty phrases so that other people could buy and use them for their own purposes.

Although Father no longer mentioned my college fund, that very absence, along with his false show of affection, made me think that something else was on his mind. There was also something very suspicious about his frequent grins, which reminded me of Mr. Dixon, the store-owner.

This suspicion was fortified one day when, coming home

from paper delivery, I saw a man, not from Laurinville, walking around our house with a clipboard in his hand. Apparently he had been inside, too, because he told me that he had my father's permission to look inside.

"I am a residential assessment specialist," the man said when I asked him what he was doing, since we had been told to always look out for the strangers. "Your father asked me to come and look at your house for assessment."

I didn't know what a residential assessment specialist was all about or what he was doing. But I didn't like the man's presence at our house. I could see on his clipboard what appeared to be the diagram of our house. The dimensions of the rooms had been written down. What appeared to be my room had "11 x 14" written on it. I just stood there and watched him unhappily.

The man walked around the house for the next twenty minutes or so, writing down his observations on the clipboard as he did so, feeling the paint on the walls and inspecting the roof and the fireplace chimney among other parts of the house. Then apparently he had finished his work.

"It's in pretty good shape for the age," the man said as he was getting ready to leave. "It should fetch a good price on the market."

Then he drove away.

Chapter Fourteen

Three days after the residential assessment specialist had come and gone, the day the whole town had been waiting for was upon us.

School was canceled and most stores, including Mr. Dixon's, closed to celebrate the 100th day of the Green Palmers and honor the war heroes. There were speeches and parades, music and dance, all day at the park. At the school auditorium that night the day would end with its final explosion of celebration. Everywhere in Laurinville was festivity and excitement, and everyone laughed and danced.

Since it was also Sunday I replaced Mother's old flowers with the very best, freshly cut new ones. They had been bought the night before at Mr. Dixon's and were kept watered through the night. Father went to the cemetery with me, now a rare occurrence. It seemed to be a special day for everyone.

The only person who was not caught up in the festive mood was Mr. Yalta, who kept muttering his favorite saying, "it's terrible, it's terrible." Even Miss Casey wore a nice dress and looked prettier than ever, ready for the celebration. She and Father danced at the park to the applause of the crowd.

As for me, it turned out to be the most significant day of my life.

It was late in the afternoon when I came home from the park to have early dinner with Father and get ready for the night's events at the auditorium. He had received a charter member's special ribbon to be placed on his lapel, which made him look distinguished and proud. He was obviously looking forward to it.

When I got near home, the first thing I noticed was a car parked in front of the house. I recognized it as the one belonging to the residential assessment specialist. The second thing I noticed was a big sign in the front yard that said "HOME FOR SALE" with someone's telephone number below it. The sign obviously meant the owner was selling his house. The third thing I noticed was the residential assessment specialist himself. He was putting on the finishing touch at the base of the signpost, stepping on the dirt around it and looking at it from different angles to make sure it was straight.

What I saw, all three things, when I realized what they all meant, took my breath away. My father was selling the house so that he could invest the money for his wealth and fortune! Ever since I had seen the residential assessment specialist, or whatever he was called, I meant to ask Father what was going on. But because of the big celebration raging all over the town I had forgotten about it. No wonder he had been so nice! All along, he had been planning to sell our house!

I started running to the house as fast as I could. It was the shock of seeing our house on sale, not the running, that made my breathing difficult as if I had been running a hundred miles. When I got to the house I found myself unable to speak.

"What, what—" I fumbled and, after some effort, managed to cry out, "what are you doing?" The man, who seemed totally unaffected by either my astonishment or the town's festivity, dusted the dirt off his hands and straightened his back a couple of times. All the while, I was trying to catch my breath.

"You are selling the house," the residential assessment

specialist simply said, "or, at least your father is."

Hearing it from that man made it worse.

"No, we are not," I shouted, "no, we are not selling the house."

"Yes, you are," the man said.

"No, we are not, no, we are not," I repeated. "My dad never told me about it, and we are not selling this house. You are wrong, mister. We are not selling."

The man stared at me lazily as if he was waiting for me to wear myself out. As I continued my protest he became impatient. He reached inside his coat pocket and pulled out a sheaf of papers and held it under my face. I refused to look.

"This is the real estate contract," the man said, waving it in my face a couple of times and putting it back in his pocket. "Your father signed it the other day."

Exhausted from my own fruitless protesting, I sat down on the door steps and, burying my face, started crying. The man stood next to me for a long time and let out a deep sigh as if he hated either my obstinacy or what he was doing.

"Well, son," he said with an effort as he started gathering up his digging tools, "you'd better have a talk with your father. He wants to sell the house and invest the money. He has to; he has already promised it to the Green Palmers. You can never get out of that."

He put the emphasis on the last word.

"Go away," I said through my tears. "You're lying. My father would never do that."

I was born in that house, and Mother died in it, too. There was no way Father was going to sell it to please the Green Palmers. Where were we going to live?

The residential assessment specialist shook his head and slowly loaded up his belongings onto his car.

"That's the Green Palmers for you," he said as if to himself. "No one can escape them once you sell your soul to them."

With that the man drove away.

As soon as the man left I sprang to action. I rushed over to the signpost and tried to pull it out. But it had been posted by a residential assessment specialist who knew how to plant a signpost. It would not budge. I tried some more but did not succeed. Panting and grunting, I kicked it and punched it with all my strength.

Then I felt a strong hand pulling me up. When I turned around, I saw Father.

"What are you doing?" he said in a strange, thick tone such as I had never heard coming out of him before. His eyes were blazing with a deadly seriousness.

I freed myself from him and went back to my attack, crying out, "you can't sell this house."

"Stop it, Mikey, stop it," he hollered.

But I would not stop.

Father tried to pull me back again, this time with greater strength. When I could no longer be restrained, he boxed my right ear from behind with fair force. The impact made me deaf in that ear, and I soon staggered and fell down. He picked me up and, turning me around to face him, gave me another good one across the face.

All the while, Father muttered: "Too late, Mikey, the Green Palmers got me. The Green Palmers got me."

My head was ringing and eyes were smarting from the blows. I jerked violently to free myself from him and, as he lost his grip, I ran inside the house. Driven by mad confusion and instinct for safety and crying incoherently, I dashed upstairs at great speed.

My room had never had a lock on the door, a fact I now

bitterly regretted as I slammed the door shut. Father soon followed me into the house, still muttering, "the Green Palmers got me." I heard him climb up the stairs. With nothing else I could do, I pulled the door shut one more time and leaned against it with all my strength.

Father was now up the stairs and at the door. I could hear his breathing and muttering about the Green Palmers. He kicked the door a couple of times. Then, obviously realizing that the door had never had a lock, he turned the knob and pushed the door open with great force.

The door was flung open and I was thrown clear across the room staggering on my feet toward the bed. Father walked into my room like a man I had never known before. His eyes were unfocused, his face expressionless, and his speech disjointed. I crawled across the bed as fast as I could and, wedged between the bed and the dresser, made myself into as small a ball as my body would allow. Between the two pieces of furniture that had been with me all my life I was absolutely cornered by my own father into an impossible situation. I held up both hands and covered my head in anticipation of his blows.

"The Green Palmers got me," Father kept saying as he walked around the bed. As he got to the foot of the bed, he lifted the corner and moved it to give himself more room. I made myself into a smaller ball and pushed myself farther into the corner. I was surprised at how small I could make myself.

Father approached me slowly and, as he got close enough, delivered his first blow to my head. Much of it landed on my wrists that covered my head, but it was painful enough for me. Then he delivered another one, then another one, then another one. I was afraid he might kick me where I had no protection, but he didn't. No doubt, he was too preoccupied with the Green Palmers to think about where to attack.

Yet, if nothing else, I thought he was going break my wrists. Then I realized that his blows were rather mechanical, as if his mind was not concentrating on what he was doing. He seemed to be going through the motion without consideration for maximum effect. His blows did not have the sting or the precision of the earlier ones that I had received outside. I began to feel optimistic about the chances for my survival.

Instinctively I decided to distribute his blows more evenly across my body by shifting my position, which turned out to be a crucial decision. Thus, when I turned to the side a little I felt something next to the wall. It was the picture frame from Mr. Yalta that I had not hung back on the wall after it had fallen off the hook. It was the only object around that could be of any use. Without thinking, I picked it up and held it in front of me. The frame was large enough, or I was small enough, for it to cover much of my body.

Since the frame contained glass, it was a risky venture to shield myself from the physical blows of my father, who had obviously lost his mind. If Father had smashed through the glass, the end-result might have been bad for both of us, perhaps worse for me since I would have had to endure the wrath of a bleeding man. Perhaps sensing the danger posed by shattered glass, Father was persuaded to stop the blows for the moment until he removed the shield from me. Whatever the reason, his blows suddenly stopped. There was a moment of confused silence. Then, shattering the silence, there was the most awful choking sound I had ever heard. It was from Father. He sounded like a man who was suddenly deprived of his breathing air, but struggling to live. I felt safe or curious enough to raise my head above the frame to take a look.

The sight was horrible. Father was clutching his throat with both hands, as if trying to choke himself to death. His eyes were wide open, bulging and ready to pop out of their sockets, and without focus. His tongue was stretched out as far as it could, as if trying to suck in as much precious air as possible. His face was red and blue and white by turns from the terrible contortion. Watching him, I was too terrified and fascinated to utter a word or move an inch. The only thought that crossed my mind at the moment was that Father was now too sick to deliver any more blows to my head.

Unable to maintain his balance any longer in his current state of health, however, he staggered sideways and crashed onto my bed. The whole house seemed to shake. A violent spasm followed, then his whole body went rigid and straight from head to toe. His face went redder, bluer and whiter with the convulsive exertion. Then he started heaving and, finally, shrieking with a most frightening gurgle I had ever heard, began to vomit a whole sea of slimy substance on my bed. The vomit came several times in rapid succession. I had no idea that even a grownup could throw up so much.

It was green slime, the vilest kind that the human mind is capable of imagining and describing, that still haunts me in my dreams sometimes. The green slime was mixed with air bubbles and specks of darker matters. The substance, as it poured out of Father's mouth like molten lava from a volcano, oozed lazily to the edge of the bed and started dripping onto the floor. Not only was it an ungainly sight, but it smelled so utterly foul that I almost fainted from its odor. The room was now filled with his gurgling and vomiting. The bubbles in the slime now and then popped, releasing yet more foul smell. Not the least impressive was the sound of the green slimy vomit dropping on to the floor in big clumps one on top of the other. As if that wasn't enough, Father rolled over on the side where his vomit was collecting, splattering the mass yet more all over the bed, the floor and himself. The sound of the slime being flattened under his weight and much of it being squirted out over great distance in many directions, some even landing on the walls, was something that I would never forget.

It was a horrid spectacle for anyone, especially for a twelve-year old boy who had grown up in genteel Laurinville. The reader might feel that, with such a fairly detailed recollection, I must have been pretty calm and collected throughout the whole experience. No, obviously not. It is only with much time and distance from the event that I can now describe it with reasonable calm and accuracy. All that I remember doing during my father's struggle for his own life was hollering and screaming with no particularly intelligible words formed in the process.

After what might have been an interminable lapse of time and struggle Father's body finally relaxed. His breathing returned to normal. His face also started returning to its normal color. Needless to say, my own breathing, and perhaps my own color, returned to normal, too.

The whole scene actually took but a few minutes. I was still clutching the frame in both hands for my dear life. Father's spectacle was so horrible that my hands ached from clutching the frame in great awe. The worst seemed over, and as his body relaxed, so did I with my hands. I put the frame down on the floor against the dresser.

Father then managed to open his lifeless eyes and saw the frame. "LIBERTY AND JUSTICE FOR ALL" was staring at him at eye level, right in front of his face. He seemed startled once again, went into a rigid state for a few more seconds while choking and gurgling somewhat, and then relaxed completely.

His eyes opened again and, with a greater focus this time, stared at the frame as if he was reading the words. His lips moved. They were silently mouthing the words "LIBERTY AND JUSTICE FOR ALL."

"Mikey," he looked at me in his sorry state and barely whispered: "Forgive me, son. Forgive me."

He was Father again. The wild, unfocused look about him had left him. He was that patient, quiet man who was my father once again. He repeated "forgive me" several times before falling into a deep sleep. His face, in spite of the green slime all over, was peaceful and content as I had always known it before the Green Palmers.

The next hour or so I exhausted myself cleaning up the mess. I took his shirt off and washed him with a wet towel as best as I could. Father was snoring loudly as if he had not slept in many days. As I was wiping his hands, I did a happy double take.

His palms were no longer green!

Chapter Fifteen

For the next two hours or so Father slept like a baby.

I opened the windows to let the fresh air into the room. With the main bulk of the mess now cleaned up, the breeze slowly returned the room to normal. I sat on the bed next to Father, watching him in peaceful sleep. He was now snoring lightly as he always did after a hard day at work.

How long has it been, the thought occurred to me, since I had felt his comforting presence? It seemed like just yesterday, or just as easily another lifetime. Or another place, other than our Laurinville where everything I had known suddenly was no more. All the people and thoughts that I had trusted and taken for granted were no more to be trusted and taken for granted. The promises that the Green Palmers had offered our town made everyone excited and evil, turning friends into foes and otherwise good people into mad wealth hunters and fortune speculators. Few remained recognizable as the people I knew and loved. But my father was back and there was hope.

My mind wandered here and there aimlessly. Then, feeling the exhaustion from the ordeal that I had just experienced, I slumped and soon drifted to sleep.

I was awakened by a sudden thunder of explosion. Looking outside, I saw the sky light up with fireworks that sprayed brilliant sparks and colors. There followed several more bursts one after the other, spreading incandescent lights and smoke trails. While I was fascinated by the fireworks, there was a knock on the door downstairs. I was trying to distinguish the knock from the fireworks and also to fully wake up. I heard the knock again.

"Mikey," a woman's voice called my name, then again, "Mikey, Mr. Brown, are you home?"

It was Miss Casey. As I managed to drag my feet downstairs, I saw her standing just inside the door still wearing the pretty dress I had seen during the day at the park.

"The door was open," she explained, pointing to it. "So I let myself in."

Darkness had fallen outside, broken now and then by the continuing thunder and lightning of fireworks. Obviously they were coming from the direction of the school where the celebration was taking place.

"I am sorry, Miss Casey," I apologized. "I didn't hear the knock because of the fireworks."

"You didn't show up," she said, looking at me suspiciously. "I thought I would come over and see what was going on. Is everything all right?"

I said everything was all right. But my voice was quivering. The ordeal of the afternoon came back alive. She sensed that something was amiss and gave me a silent hug.

I broke down and cried. She led me to the kitchen and switched on the light to take a better look at me. What she saw must not have been a pretty sight because she let out a small gasp of alarm. My face and arms were black and blue, and my clothes were soiled with the green slime. I had cleaned up Father reasonably but I had forgotten about myself. Miss Casey demanded an explanation as she went about washing me up in the kitchen.

Between sobs and blowing my nose I told her everything that had happened. The sale signpost, the struggle with Father, the picture frame, and finally the massive green slime Father had spewed on my bed. She gave me another reassuring hug and prodded me to lead her upstairs to the scene of the most unusual phenomenon.

Thankfully the room had lost most of that foul odor. In fact, it was even pleasant in the cool breeze of the early fall. Father was still deep in sleep, continuing his light snoring.

"Is that the thing that saved you?" she asked, pointing to the frame still standing against the dresser.

I nodded. I told her that it had been a present from Mr. Yalta on America Day, which he made himself specially for me. It had been such a long time ago. Thoughtfully her eyes alternated between me and the frame several times. Then, making sure that everything was all right with my father and complimenting me on my excellent clean-up job, Miss Casey set to work putting the room back in order.

She drew bath water for me while she changed the bed spread. The water felt wonderful. I noticed the aches and pains from Father's blows beginning to throb for the first time as I soacked. But it felt so good to be in the tub and to hear Miss Casey's efficient movement about, like part of the family, that I even splashed the water a little and wished for some bath toys.

The booming sounds of fireworks continued a while longer, indicating that the hour of the main event was nearing. The auditorium was not too far from our house. (Nothing in Laurinville is too far from anything.) I could hear the townspeople chatting and laughing between the booms of fireworks. They were on their way to the auditorium to commemorate the 100th day of the Green Palmers. My thought drifted to the auditorium I helped decorate. Then I thought about the scene of money-eating as Greg and John had described it, which might be the highlight of the evening's celebration.

But it was when I was watching Miss Casey trying to hang the frame back on the wall, but failing twice and giving up on it, that I had a thought like a lightning bolt across a dark sky. The idea was daring but also absurd even for a boy whose youth may forgive much absurdity. In fact, it was so absurd that I didn't think I could tell anyone, not even Miss Casey. But I had to try it.

Galvanized by the idea, I quickly got out of the tub, dried and dressed in clean clothes. There was no time to appreciate even the simple pleasure of putting on clean clothes after the ordeal with Father's slime. Miss Casey, who had succeeded in putting back to some semblance of respectability into my room, was sitting on the edge of the bed watching the sleeping man. If I had not been so preoccupied with an idea or in such a hurry at the moment, I might have been impressed by the sweet and reassuring presence that Miss Casey was casting upon our household. She was holding Father's hand, which would have been scandalous under other circumstances. But it had been an extraordinary event and, besides, I had no time to think about the finer points of life.

I went for the picture frame. After failing to put it back up on the wall, Miss Casey had left the frame back on the floor. I picked it up and headed for the door.

"What are you doing with that, Mikey?" she inquired. "And where are you going?"

Father reacted to the voices by barely opening one eye and trying to see through it. This he didn't seem to manage very well, because he didn't stir.

"I'm going to the auditorium, Miss Casey," I said. "I'm going to celebrate the Green Palmers' Day, like everybody else in town."

She looked at me and at the picture frame in some confusion while repeatedly saying "why?"

"I'm sorry, Miss Casey, but I can't tell you right now," I apologized and, with the frame under my arm, bolted out the door. It might have been my imagination, but I thought I saw an expression of understanding registering on Miss Casey's face. Then the understanding was transformed instantly into a flicker of alarm. She called after me a couple of times after me as I ran downstairs and out the door.

The fireworks had ended, which meant the celebration was already under way. There were still some townspeople walking toward the auditorium. Some of them recognized me and inquired about what I was carrying. By then I was practically running, and managed only barely polite answers.

As I neared the school, I began to hear the swelling roar of the crowd from the auditorium. All the lights had been turned on, such as I had never seen before at our school. There had been more decorations added to the buildings since I had seen them last. Long, spiral green ribbons draped down from a point at the top of each building, down to the nearest pine trees, where they were tied off. Banners showing the Green Palm had been put up on the front sides of the buildings, brightly lit by three flood lights. A large placard placed above all the other signs and banners and ribbons said, "WELCOME TO GREEN PALMER DAY CELEBRATION."

The lights and decorations, and the crowd noise, had changed my school into something altogether foreign. It reminded me of the circus that had come to Laurinville when I was six which I had gone to see with my parents. I was amazed that an ordinary country school could change so quickly into something so different.

As I got near the auditorium, the noise and speech-making swelled to a higher level. The celebration had been going on for some time. Two or three boys, obviously against the wishes of their parents, were hiding outside trying to listen in. I recognized the boys who put their fingers to their lips for silence. I nodded in agreement and passed them by hurriedly.

The main entrance to the auditorium, which opened to the

hallway with doors at both ends, was open. In contrast to the blazing lights inside, the hallway was relatively dark. Only two small lights shone dimly from the ceiling. I had been to the auditorium many times before, but never at night. The noise and lights temporarily distracted me from my sense of familiarity. I went through one of the side entrances and walked toward the main door.

As I stood at the main entrance, the sight virtually blinded me. Apparently the military celebration had already taken place because the heroes of the War of the Reservoir were seated with a bundle of flowers in their arms. Those who were war heroes *and* charter members were seated, with bundles of flowers in their arms. Just about everyone from Laurinville seemed to be there. (Miss Raynor's chronicle records that 91 percent of Laurinville's healthy adults were present in the auditorium at the time. But, to me, it could easily have been 100 percent.)

Half a dozen or so Green Palmers in their smart suits were about ready to commence the main part of the celebration. They stood in the front, holding the boxes that presumably contained the dirtiest dollar bills in circulation. The screen had already been pulled down for the showing of all the germs and fungi and viruses that collected on dollar bills. Greg and John had given me such a vivid description of their money-eating ritual that I could guess that the event was about to take place. The crowd seemed restless and excited with anticipation.

I held the picture frame in front of me, standing it up so that the writing was clearly visible to everyone. Clutching the bottom of the frame with my right hand, and the top with my left, and breathlessly reciting to myself "libertyandjusticeforalllibertyandjusticeforalllibertyandjusticeforall…" like a memorized prayer, I took a trembling step into the auditorium.

For a second or two there was a deafening silence. Or

perhaps it was my ears which had temporarily stopped hearing anything. I held up the frame higher as my recitation became louder. Then I moved the frame slowly side to side like an electric fan, with emphasis on the Green Palmers on the floor, to make sure that everyone could read "LIBERTY AND JUSTICE FOR ALL."

Pandemonium broke out. The crowd reacted as if it was suddenly engulfed in smoke, choking and coughing, clutching their throats. The Green Palmers turned their heads away from me and, holding their hands up as if to protect themselves from something terribly painful, hollered: "Get that boy! Get that boy!"

But nobody was in a mood to move against me. I was now unafraid of what they might do. Recalling what I had seen earlier in Father's reaction made me feel brave. Besides, every person there was trying to save himself from the awesome forces of liberty and justice for all.

Suddenly, like the typical young boy I was, I felt the surge of my own power against evil. Feeling the power and deciding to turn up the strength especially for the Green Palmers, I confidently took several steps forward toward them. They were now desperately covering up and turning their faces away in agony. In the process, however, my triumph instantly turned to disaster: I tripped over an electric cable on the floor and fell on my face. The picture frame went flying and landed on the floor a foot or so away from my outstretched hands.

My foolish misfortune altered everything. The Green Palmers lost no time in taking advantage of the situation. One of them rushed over and instantly jumped on the picture frame. The sound of the glass breaking under his crushing feet was like a summer shower on a dry garden. It immediately relieved the crowd of their choking and coughing. Revived, and straightening themselves out in general, the crowd sat back down in their seats in anticipation of the next spectacle.

The man who had jumped on the frame then shifted his direction and sat down on me with his whole weight. He held my hair in his hand and made sure that my face was in contact with the floor. For good measure he bashed my face against the hard floor several times. It was the second time within a span of few hours that I was attacked by a grownup. The cold floor, however, took some of the heat I felt in my face.

"Aha, here is our Mr. Michael Brown," the Green Palmer said triumphantly, raising my head by my hair, so that everyone could see me. "So he wanted to be a hero, I see."

He stood up, relieving me of his great weight, still clutching my hair in his hand, which meant that I had to get up from the floor with him. The man pushed me ahead of him and walked me to the center of the stage.

"Ladies and gentlemen," the man hollered to the crowd, "may I introduce you to Michael Brown, a brave young man. Tonight, we are going to make him our newest and youngest Green Palmer!"

The crowd cheered and I fainted. The last thought I had was what the dirtiest dollar bill would taste like in my mouth.

Chapter Sixteen

I regained consciousness to the most revolting smell that had ever been thrust into my nostrils.

When I came to, I found myself shuddering violently against the source of the smell held so closely to my nose. No, it was not the smelling salts normally used to revive people.

It was a dollar bill, a dirty old dollar bill that somebody was pushing against my nose.

Although most people use money every day, buying things with it and carrying it in their wallets and pocketbooks, almost no one ever smells it. I know there are people who kiss it, especially in a moment of extreme delight produced by money, even enjoying the brief contact with it or thrusting it into their bosom for convenience. But smelling it is something else entirely. I challenge the reader to find a dirty old bill, preferably a one dollar bill because it travels more widely than the other denominations, and try to smell it. The smell from it has easily convinced me that we are indeed blessed by not having a dog's acute sense of smell.

The odor of the dollar bill thrust against my nostrils produced a violent reaction from me. To be sure, it revived me instantly but also made me gag with its revolting peculiarity. The smell was indescribably foul. All the different body odors, sweat glands, germs, fungi, viruses, saliva, skin diseases, waste products, decaying food materials, etc., etc., of the hundreds of people who had ever touched the money were mercilessly attacking my sensitive nose. I would have had to be dead or near dead not to be jerked back to life by such a violent assault on my sensitivity. The combined smell of the vilest collection of human excretion, contributed by so many, concentrated on the singular object under my nose almost made me faint again. It was like no other odor. It was none that I could readily recognize. No wonder, for the foul smell from the money was not only a combination of all those vile mixtures. It was also what statisticians call a "permutation" of such mixed substances, because the mixtures created their own *new* elements entirely foreign to our normal experience.

The Green Palmers were obviously aware of the violent revulsion that the bill was capable of producing in human beings. For my benefit, they put their knowledge to good effect. Within a minute or so under the toxic administration, I was fully revived. However, it was only my senses that were revived and liberated. My body was still held captive by the Green Palmers. Two of them held tightly onto me, one on each side, twisting my arms slightly backwards, so that I lost all freedom to move. A third man, perhaps the one who had jumped on the picture frame, was still clutching my hair so that I could not move my head.

Recalling the report from Greg and John, I knew what was coming next. In a low voice, one of the Green Palmers started singing something that resembled a religious song.

"Let us commence our ceremony," a Green Palmer who seemed to be in charge said loudly enough to be heard above the singing. The audience closed their eyes. Virtually everyone from Laurinville was there. Mayor Miller with his green ribbon tied diagonally across his chest, Mr. Anderson with a new medal pinned to his chest standing next his commander-in-chief, Mr. LaGrange, Mr. McNamee, Chief Rogers and his deputy, Mr. Shepeck with hair neatly combed, Coach Sabella in his jogging suit and a baseball hat, Mr. Willis and Mr. Dixon, among others, were all there, with the dollar bill held in their hands.

"Oh, All Mighty Green Palm," the leader said in a beautiful sing-song voice, which was quite hypnotic, "bless the followers, particularly our youngest new member tonight, who are about to recommit themselves to wealth, fortune, and the Green Palm Way of Life."

With that, they all turned their bills long ways and, thrusting the bills into their mouths like racoon dogs with snakes, started chewing the money from the corner.

Different people make different sounds when they eat. Also different food substances make different sounds when they are eaten. The sound of drinking water is different from the sound of drinking soda. The sound of chewing a sandwich is different from the sound of chewing apple pie. By listening to the peculiar sound quality, observant people can tell what kind of food is being eaten. But these people would be completely stumped and confounded by their inability to guess when the food being eaten is an old dollar bill. They would be even more at a loss when so many people chew their dirty dollar bills all at the same time.

The sound of dollar bills being chewed was unlike any other chewing sound that I had ever heard. Obviously I had never heard dollar bills chewed by so many people at the same time in a relatively small and quiet auditorium. It was the most ghastly noise. The material that goes into making the bills, half fabric and half paper, is unlike any substance ever chewed between the human teeth. It is a totally baffling sound new to our hearing experience. The sound it creates is easily the most revolting acoustic sensation ever visited upon the human ear.

Although the third man tried to hold my head down, I managed to watch the money-eaters at the peak of their chewing activity. It appeared that some of them were only mildly enthusiastic about what they had to eat. They lacked appropriate vigor in their jaw movements, because they chewed it rather fast and swallowed it quickly.

But the majority of them seemed to be new to the experience. They chewed their bills slowly and deliberately as if committing the taste to eternal memory. Saliva was leaking through the corners of their mouths, running down on their chests. Their saliva was obviously greenish, mixed with ink, which soiled their fine clothes in a most dramatic fashion. The sight was horrible as well as fascinating. Nearly nine hundred people stood there as if in a spinach-tasting contest, chewing the green stuff in utmost concentration. Their green mouths moved like the mouths of cows on the meadow indulging in their silent grazing. Because the ink that prints the money was now freshly exposed in the process, an entirely different kind of odor filled the auditorium.

The third man, discovering that I had been watching the crowd, violently pushed my head down. I hollered in pain. Thereafter, I could only hear the chewing and smell its pungent ink odor. After what appeared to be an eternity, all was quiet once again and everyone was seated. I assumed their palms had all turned green by now but I could not confirm it.

"Ladies and gentlemen," the leader raised his hands and called for attention from the crowd. "Now is the moment we have all been waiting for. Mr. Michael Brown will be initiated into the blessings of the Green Palm. Would you please bring me the special dollar bill for Mr. Brown?" A man brought a dollar bill over to him, which the leader held in his hand and raised above his head for the crowd to see.

"Here is the most blessed dollar bill in existence," the man declared in his sing-song voice. "It has been touched by every skin disease known to mankind, suffered by thousands of people from all corners of the world. This is only one of its kind. Indeed, blessed is the one who is about to commit himself to the most exalted realm of existence, etc., etc."

Everyone, even the men holding me, was mesmerized by the famous dollar bill that was about to be administered to a boy. Their grip seemed to be loosening somewhat. Recognizing that split-second advantage, I made my survival move. I shook their hands off with all my strength and bolted for the main door. In surprise, some of them even parted to let me go through.

But I was one step too slow. A Green Palmer was already there, blocking the door. Not knowing what else to do, I turned and ran down the side of the auditorium through a narrow passage between the arranged chairs and the wall. To slow down my pursuers, I kicked and slammed every object that I could reach in their general direction. All the while I was hollering: "Help me! Help me!"

But nobody in the crowd moved, neither to stop me nor to help me. They just sat there and watched me and my pursuers with no particular interest or amusement. As I turned the corner and ran across the back of the auditorium, I knew I was going to be cornered. The Green Palmers were behind me, ahead of me, and waiting for me at the other end.

I had no other choice. Abruptly stopping my run, I jumped over the last rows of people in a wild dash for survival. I was still screaming for help, but no one moved to help me. However, they did instinctively make room for me to run through. Too big to run through the seats to catch me, the Green Palmers stood just outside waiting for me. I was like a hunted rabbit.

At the end I was too exhausted to move. It was not easy to move about between seats and the many pairs of adult knees. I simply stopped in the middle of the crowd where I felt the safest, panting. I looked up at the nearest person there and saw that it was Mr. Rogers, the police chief.

The leader had apparently recognized this crucial fact that was possibly to his advantage.

"Chief!" he ordered with authority. "Arrest that boy!"

To my amazement, the chief of police did exactly that. He quietly stood up, picked me up by the waist, and calmly waded through the seats to deliver me to my pursuers. I did not resist the arresting officer of the law who was merely doing his job. The Green Palmers eagerly pounced on me and dragged me, tightly secured, back to the center of the stage. They pulled my arms back so hard that I thought my shoulders were going to pop out of their sockets.

I was positioned once again, as if nothing had happened to interrupt the proceedings, facing the ordeal of eating the dirtiest dollar bill ever in existence. The leader repeated some of the earlier incantation, including the qualifications of the dollar bill as unique in the world. Then he stood in front of me with the obvious intention of feeding me the money. On cue, a man jerked my head back to raise my face toward the leader with the dollar bill and pulled my jaws down to open my mouth.

"Now, boy," he whispered, bringing his face close to mine: "Eat it and be blessed! You will become one of us!"

There was little room for me to move my head to avoid the object. The vilest dollar bill, touched by every known skin disease, reeking the rottenest odor I had ever encountered, was within an inch of my mouth. I struggled with all my strength.

"Eat it!" the man ordered.

There was only one remaining thing that I could do. I

summoned my remaining strength and yelled as loudly as I had ever yelled in my life: "LIBERTY AND JUSTICE FOR ALL!"

The words did not come out exactly right because of the awkward way the man kept my jaws down and the dryness in my throat. But the words had an impact, because their grip on me loosened up just a tad. Then the echo of my yell died down. I was so exhausted that even yelling those words out took all my strength. Panting for air, I gathered my breath for another yell. But even before I could say "liberty," one of the Green Palmers standing nearby slapped my mouth hard. I thought my lips had exploded.

That hard slap shut me up for good. There was no more strength left in me. I could recite "libertyandjusticeforall" only in my own mind.

"Liberty and justice for all, uh?" the leader mocked my last effort with a smirk. "Indeed! But, young man, what's liberty if it's not just for you? What's justice if it doesn't serve just you? Liberty and justice for *all*! Who cares about liberty or justice unless it's just for you, you alone, and nobody else? Now, you're about to learn the Green Palm Way of liberty and justice."

The man said the last sentence loudly enough to be heard by all. There was a huge outburst of laughter that rocked the auditorium.

It was hopeless. I was too tired to move. I told myself that all I had to do was open my mouth and accept the money and give it one big swallow, and it would be over. I stopped fighting.

I raised my face to the man and obediently opened my mouth.

"Good boy," the leading Green Palmer smiled sweetly and whispered to me. "You will be happy just like your father and all the rest in this town who committed their souls to the Green

Palm. May the Green Palm Way bring you all your wealth and fortune—."

As he was about to thrust the vile object into my tired mouth, the man stopped in mid-air as if suddenly frozen. The Green Palmers who had been holding me up did likewise, dropping me onto the floor like a sack of potatoes.

I managed to look up at the source of the new commotion.

Three people had just entered the auditorium, each one holding a sign that read: "LIBERTY AND JUSTICE FOR ALL."

Oh, how sweet to read those words! Oh, how wonderful to see Father, Miss Casey, and Mr. Yalta, each holding a sign, so proudly and so straight!

Amid the now familiar sounds of gurgling and choking all around me, I fainted one more time.

Chapter Seventeen

When I finally regained consciousness I found myself seated on the front row among the Charter Members and the heroes of the war. I wasn't sure how long I had been out.

"Here you are," the leading Green Palmer said brightly, as he recognized that I had regained myself. "Would you please come forward to the front so that everyone can see you?"

I wanted to protest that I didn't want to, but could not say a word. My throat was dry and my mouth swollen shut. Then the horrible thought occurred to me that I might have after all eaten the money. The revolting thought made me want to throw up in disgust. My body was so tired from the day's experiences that I could not control one single muscle. It would simply refuse to obey my command.

But why isn't Father helping me? What happened to Miss Casey and Mr. Yalta who walked in with their signs? I desperately wanted to know. To my shock, as I looked around to find them, I saw that they were all there among the front-row members—Father, Miss Casey, and Mr. Yalta. They were all grinning at me as if I had done something wonderful and they were proud of it. Their signs, broken and obviously stepped on, lay on the floor near their feet. Oh, my God, I said to myself, the Green Palmers got them! We had lost.

"Mikey," the leader, seeing that I was not moving, called my name sweetly, "come forward. Don't be afraid. You are now one of us."

There was something wickedly confident in the man's manner, as if he knew he had me cornered. In mounting horror and disbelief, and eyes closed, I slowly raised my hands to my face and opened my eyes.

Horror of horrors, my palms were green!

I had become a Green Palmer! In acknowledgement of that fact, the crowd in the auditorium roared with approval. I saw Father, Miss Casey and Mr. Yalta vigorously clapping their hands. Their palms were all green, too.

"Come on, Mikey," the leading man said sweetly again. "It's too late, now. You are one of us. You can never underestimate the powers of the Green Palm Way. It always gets you in the end. It always gets you."

I stood up slowly as the crowd roared louder and walked toward the leader. He took my arm and led me to the center of the stage. There I was, under their control, once again unable to do anything about it.

"Ladies and gentlemen," the leading man said in his beautiful sing-song voice, "may I introduce you our youngest and newest member of the Green Palm family?"

The crowd roared and the auditorium rocked with noise.

"Now, Mikey," the man whispered close to my ear as everyone became suddenly quiet. "As a Green Palmer you can get anything you want. You don't have to do any homework if you don't want to. You can steal somebody else's lunch or pocket-money. You can be as lazy as you want to be. Anything you want to do, you can do. Anything you want to get, you can get. You want money? You can have it. You want to do something nasty to somebody? You can do that, too. You are a

Green Palmer, now, and that's the Green Palm Way."

The man was talking to me so sweetly and so lovingly that I was thinking to myself, Why is this man so good to me?

The man somehow knew what I was thinking.

"Because we love you, and we care for you," he whispered. "Because we love you, and we care for you, we want to give you anything you want, anything your heart desires. After all, that is the Green Palm Way."

What do I have to do to get everything I want? I was asking him again in my thought. The man heard my thought.

He picked up a box that was laying on the floor in front of him. He pulled out some more dollar bills, maybe five or so, and held them up for me to see. They were dirty old dollar bills again.

The man lowered his whisper, getting closer to my ear: "All you have to do is eat some more money."

Then he put the money in my hand and said: "Now, just put it into your mouth and swallow it. Just do it, and all your dreams will come true. Everything you have ever wanted, everything you have ever desired. All the playthings at Toys 'R' Me, all the tele-mind you ever wanted to watch, all the bad things you ever wanted to do to other kids, all the lies you ever wanted to tell…"

I looked at the money in my hand for a while and looked around. Everyone in the auditorium, including Father, Miss Casey and Mr. Yalta, was nodding to me, encouraging me to go ahead and eat the money.

I have already eaten one, I thought to myself. Why can't I eat some more?

The leading Green Palmer whispered to me again, reading my thought: "Yes, Mikey, what's some more money to eat? You just get more blessings of the Green Palm Way. Yes, Mikey, go ahead."

THE GREEN PALMERS

Then the whole crowd began whispering: "Yes, Mikey, go ahead. Yes, Mikey, go ahead." It was a terrifying moment of indecision for me. Something inside me said it was all right for me to do it. Something else said it was not all right.

But, in the end, the powers of the Green Palm proved too much for me to resist. I put the money into my mouth and started to chew.

But apparently I had misjudged my taste-buds. The taste of the money was so revolting that I felt as if my head was exploding. There was no way I could do it.

Gagging and choking in my dry throat, I spat the money out. If I had already become a Green Palmer, God forgive me, I didn't want any more Green Palm blessings. I wanted to scream for help.

But no one there in the auditorium would help me. I wanted my mother. I desperately wanted her to come and help me.

"Help me, Mom! Help me!" I screamed as loudly as I could with my swollen mouth and dry throat. "I don't want to be a Green Palmer. Help me!"

Getting those words out was not easy. But I was trying as if my life depended on it. The leading Green Palmer straightened himself and stood up.

"Obviously, Mikey needs some more convincing," he said, without sounding too disappointed or displeased, mostly to the other Green Palmers around him. "Take him to the next room and we will see how long he can hold out and resist the greater blessings of the Green Palm Way."

The two men who had earlier held my arms came forward and, holding my arms again, this time not too tightly, led me to a smaller room just outside the main entrance to the auditorium. The room was dark but surprisingly comfortable, almost like our own living room. I had been inside virtually all of the rooms in the building but could not remember having ever been inside this one. My head was fairly unclear and my face was burning from all the abuses it had received, and thinking hard about the room only made it hurt worse. The two men gently deposited me into an easy chair. My body welcomed the comfort, after all the strenuous activity.

The leader and the other Green Palmers had followed me and positioned themselves in a semi-circle behind me. Although they had brought me into this room perhaps for some further demonstrations of the great Green Palm Way, I was too tired and comfortable to either think or look around.

"Why don't you turn it on, now?" the leader told a man. "So that our little friend can enjoy the full benefits of our Almighty Green Palm. I am sure he will enjoy it and see everything our way."

His comment made me bolt up and look. What I noticed then was a large machine, the size of one of our school vending machines, with a glass front on the side that faced me, and a row of knobs and switches next to it. I had never seen a real tele-mind set in my life, but instantly recognizing the infernal machine, my heart froze. Oh, my God, I was going to watch this thing and become a zombie!

But even before my mind was capable of understanding the full impact of this new terror, one of the men extended his hand toward the set and pushed a button on the little flat box he held in his hand. The machine came alive, sound and picture materializing together like dreamy magic. Someone in the machine said that they were going to "take a commercial break." With this announcement came on the screen a series of the most wonderful scenes I had ever seen in my life. I am somewhat ashamed to admit that I did not resist the assault from the tele-mind with all my remaining strength, though I had little left. The tele-mind was turned on, and the pictures and sounds came on so swiftly that neither my mind nor my body had any time to react. I was instantly overcome and mesmerized by the powers of tele-mind.

The so-called "commercials" took my breath away, overwhelming all my senses with their sheer wonder and beauty. In those commercials, people were unfailingly nice, smiling and loving each other. Skies were bluer than blue, and flowers in vivid and fetching colors were everywhere in full bloom. There was background music in every scene that quickened my heartbeat and made me feel exceedingly good about myself and my future. In commercials, anything bad happened could be easily resolved. In them everyone loved everyone, cared for everyone, and trusted everyone. Everything was so beautiful to watch, so exciting to have, and so delicious to eat. Some commercials were funny, some slow, some breathlessly fast, some fearful and anxious, some pathetic and pleading, depending on what was being advertised. Some of them appealed to pride, some to envy, some to laziness, some to anger, some to desire…

Everyone in the commercials looked sweet, sincere, and helpful, reminding me of the new vice president at Mr. McNamee's bank. Everything they said, did, or showed looked positively urgent, irresistible, and desirable. Nothing was ever boring in commercials. Watching them one after another, I forgot all about where I was, who I was, or what was going to happen to me. I even forgot about the Green Palmers. Tele-mind made me want to scream to the whole town of Laurinville that I was the most loved person in the world. I was the customer-king, just like the old lady pensioner at Miss Casey's shop, who could demand anything from anyone. All the commercials were worried that I was not satisfied or happy enough every minute of my life. They were worried that my hair was not clean and shiny enough, that my food was not tasty enough, that my day was not filled with enough excitement, comfort, and pleasure.

In one particular commercial there were beautiful women with much coloring on their faces, almost naked and quite friendly, asking me to call them so that we could "have a good time." A telephone number flashed on the screen as irresistibly as their smiles and winks. I looked around, wishing for a telephone nearby so that I could call them.

Then there were those toys, sneakers, games, breakfast cereals—those endless streams of wonderful things—offered by people who loved children and cared for their fun and success, urgently describing the most heavenly inventions ever made for us. Even a silly thing like brushing your teeth was important, and which those generous people worked so hard to make it so perfect and unforgettable. Every flower, every rain drop, every cloud, every face—every second—was picturesque and vivid, accompanied by music now pulsating, now serene, and now heartbreaking rhythm and melody, as if created by the most creative genius just for me.

On tele-mind, everything was easy and free, just one quick phone call or signature away. Abundant things were made available to everyone, old and young, men and women, children and pets, always offered in the most caring, exciting, and urgent manner of sweet offerings. They came and came and came.

I was in a trance, thinking I had died and gone to heaven.

Then came the main program about a young dashing hero who killed many of his enemies singlehandedly. Some of them he killed with his guns, some with bombs, some with assortments of other gadgets, and in a variety of surprisingly original and ingenuous ways. Blood spurted out of their wounds, and their agonizing and shrieking filled the screen and my eardrums. Their mutilated bodies fell to the ground or flew away in slow movement, and I could see everything in clear detail—every clump of torn flesh and every gush of blood from the victims. My own heart was pounding with excitement, forgetting all about my exhaustion and hurt, while the screen exploded with unrelenting violence, noise, and destruction.

The Green Palmer with the little box in his hand pushed another button and the scene changed instantly. The change came in the middle of a breathlessly thrilling chase action, someone's life hanging in balance, and I almost screamed with irritation at the rude interruption.

But the next scene was just as interesting, if somewhat slow. It was an election campaign and the politician was speaking to a crowd. Signs showing his name, "Bob Beezle," were everywhere. The candidate was attractive and well-spoken. He promised to deliver good things to the throng of people who cheered as he spoke. He said he would not raise taxes but everyone would be prosperous and happy if he got elected to office. The crowd was ecstatic at his promises, hollering and calling him by his first name. Balloons of different colors soared into the sky, and exciting slogans and images filled the screen. Quite in contrast, however, I noticed some solemn looking men in dark suits and wearing dark glasses, strangely out of place and seemingly unaffected by the powerfully affecting goings-on, surrounding the candidate as if he was among his mortal enemies. These men glanced around nervously and at all times kept their hands near their breast pockets which bulged with something inside. The politician pleaded that he needed their votes. His voice was strong, and his pleading for their votes irresistibly moving. I was absolutely charmed by the man's promises of good things at no cost to anyone. "I will vote for you, Bob! I love you!" I found myself screaming in uncontrollable excitement. Someone's hand was gently placed on my shoulder as if to calm me down, which I barely noticed.

In another instant the scene changed. A kind-looking and well-nourished woman appeared, showing wretchedly starving dark children in a faraway place with their thin skin stuck to the bones. After what seemed like an endless series of pictures of dying children, the woman, in a teary and cracking voice, appealed for money to send to help feed those children, in the faraway land. It was a supplication no human being with any kindness could resist. The pictures of the poor starving children and the sweet woman's appeal were so wonderfully heartbreaking that at the moment I was willing to give all my fortune to her organization. Unlike my unstoppable reaction to the political candidate, the kindhearted woman's appeal was so lovely that I began to cry, tears streaking down my cheeks. Just before it was over, a message flashed on the screen that said, "Miss Stoddard is Compensated for This Endorsement," the meaning of which I did not understand. My sadness did not last long, because the man kept changing the channels, showing me more excitement on every channel. At times I was so restless with what could be on the next channel that I found myself urging the man with the box to go to the next one, just shaking my index finger and pointing to the screen. There was a loud and bone-crunching sporting event with a large screaming crowd who admired their favorite players, calling them "our children's role models." (I was hoping to see Mitchell Jordan, Mr. Sabella's great hero but could not tell who was who. They were all wearing thickly-padded uniforms and helmets that covered most of their faces.) Then there were luxury vacations, cars, food, drinks, newspapers, and magazines, promising all kinds of heavenly things that could be delivered to me by a telephone call or a signature on a card. I could understand why everyone loved the Green Palmers.

One channel showed what they called the "Eyewitness News." An intelligent-looking man with well-combed hair smoothly moved the program from one news item to another. He showed many entertaining pictures, like a war scene with great many casualties; a "mass murderer" with a machine gun held proudly in his hands; a raging fire that burned seven people to "charred remains" as the reporter described them in great detail; a nature park accident where a crocodile bit off the arm of its handler; a five-car traffic accident; a drug trial; a bank robbery that included an exciting car chase by police; a kind woman's effort to save a tree; and other fast-moving events of the day. The last item, called "Hero of the Day," was about a college basketball coach, bespectacled and serious looking, who cried at his press conference and said, "This has been the most difficult decision for me and for my family to make." The intelligent looking "anchorman" explained that the coach had just switched the sneakers for his players from something called Adda to another company called Nicks for two million dollars. The anchorman called the coach "one of the best role models in this great nation of ours." It was so nice of them to collect all the important events so that I could sit there comfortably and learn about them. I was so sorry when the news was over and turned around to ask someone when I could watch it again. But before I could ask, the scene switched.

A handsome preacher, beautifully groomed and dressed with meticulous care (which reminded me how ugly and uncouth my father had looked after the vomiting), his teeth even and white, his smile frequent and inviting, his eyes shining with sincerity for the love of God, was preaching in inspired fervor. At his side was his wife with great flaming pink hair and a face ready for stage, casting an admiring glance at her husband. They were the best-looking couple I had ever seen in my life. The handsome preacher was saying that, according to the latest survey, 97 percent of Americans believed in God and thought of America as "a God-fearing Christian nation." The audience sitting in front of him cheered wildly at the "survey." Then he turned straight to me and said that, as a messenger of God, he loved me and cared for my happiness and well-being. But for him to continue his good work for God he needed money and he appealed to my heart and my love for God to send him the money to carry out his mission. He promised that I would be rewarded with wealth and fortune for my love of God. His words and appearance were so godly, so full of piety and hope and charity that I wanted to rush over to Mr. McNamee's bank and send all my money to the handsome preacher and his beautiful wife. I had never felt so loved and prayed for in my whole life.

Everything on tele-mind was so easy and so clear that any child could understand it and enjoy its many messages. Nothing was ever shown without pictures that made the whole thing so easy to understand. If the words were unclear, the picture made everything instantly clear. The announcement of every upcoming event was made by one with the most authoritative and dramatic voice as if God himself was announcing His Second Coming, commanding my absolute obedience. It was so awe-inspiring and attention-demanding that it brooked no second thoughts from me.

Then, in another instant, just at the peak of my ecstatic fantasy, my whole world fell rudely apart. In the middle of an incredibly joyous scene, THE MAN TURNED THE TELE-

MIND SET OFF! Zombie-like, I looked around to see if anyone could help me. From the most unrelenting supply of pleasure that I had ever experienced, I was suddenly ejected out into the cold and nothingness at the flick of a cruel button! Just like that!

I wanted it back! I wanted my beloved tele-mind back! I screamed in agony and slumped on the floor.

Chapter Eighteen

The pain of paradise disappearing in an instant was unbearable.

I picked myself up and rushed toward the man with the box and tried to snatch it away from him. The man calmly raised his hand, just high enough so that I could not reach it. I kept jumping for the box, but the most precious thing I had ever tried to touch in my whole life was just out of my reach. After several attempts, I dashed to the tele-mind set, fumbling for the switches and knobs to see any of them would make everything come back for me. All the while, I was crying and begging. The blasted set did not respond to any of my pushing and pounding. Giving up, I ran to one Green Palmer after another in frantic madness, pleading and demanding.

"Please, would you turn the tele-mind on? Please!" I pleaded with no one in particular. "I want more tele-mind! I want more tele-mind!"

None of the Green Palmers reacted to my pleading or demanding.

"Just one more commercial, please," I beseeched with all my heart. "Just one more, please!"

I was going out of my mind. My body seemed to go cold, my breathing rapid and shallow. My muscles ached as if they were being squeezed by a gigantic vice. I dropped to the floor and writhed all over, holding my head with both hands tightly trying to stop it from exploding, and crying for the tele-mind just one more time. For a little more tele-mind I would have given or done anything in the world.

"Please, I will do anything!" I told them.

On cue from the leading Green Palmer, the light in the room was switched on. He looked at me thoughtfully, although I could not see his face clearly because the light was behind him. But I could tell that there was a smile on his lips.

"Then, my boy," the leader said slowly, "would you swear that you will commit yourself wholeheartedly to the Green Palm Way of Life?"

"Yes, yes," I could not have been more eager. "Please, hurry. I want to see more tele-mind, please!"

"Not so fast, Mikey," the leading Green Palmer said, "would you also swear that you will always put your own self above all else, including your town of Laurinville, your friends, and even your family?"

I swore to him with utmost sincerity and conviction that I would. Please, just turn the tele-mind on. My thoughts were so uncontrollably rushing back to those wonderful commercials and loving people that I was trembling with powerful anticipation and impatience.

"Then, my boy," the Green Palmer said, "would you go back to the auditorium and show the people what a great Green Palmer you are and eat the dollar bills?"

I did not even answer that question. I just turned around and walked back toward the auditorium, leading the Green Palmers.

Once again, I entered the scene of my failed escape, in a fashion slightly different from my exit only a few minutes ago. But what a difference the few minutes made! Now I was coming back as a Green Palmer and a tele-minder in good standing, about to swear my allegiance to the new master.

I slumped on one of the chairs in the front row and motioned for the box that contained the dollar bills. Immediately the box was brought to me, already opened. I hurriedly grabbed the bills and was about to stuff my mouth with them when I suddenly noticed one of the broken signs staring at me. It said, "Liberty and Justice for All." It must have belonged to either Father, Miss Casey, or Mr. Yalta.

LIBERTY AND JUSTICE FOR ALL!

It seemed like an eternity ago that I had seen those words. It was another world and perhaps another Michael Brown in which those sweet words meant anything. I looked around and saw the smiling, confident faces of the Green Palmers and townspeople. Something like a surge of anger swept through my mind, and my body was set on fire.

I closed my eyes and screamed, "NOOOOOO! I WON'T DO IT! I WON'T DO IT! OH, HELP ME, SOMEBODY! HELP ME!"

"Mikey, Mikey," someone was shaking me. "Wake up!"

I struggled and finally opened my eyes in a start. Panting for breath, I was expecting to be surrounded by the Green Palmers, but it was Miss Casey's relieved face that I saw. She had been putting a wet cloth on my forehead. I found myself lying comfortably on the floor, propped up by someone's folded coat. Father and Mr. Yalta nearby rushed over and grinned at me. It was the happiest sight I had ever seen.

"Hey, there, I thought you were going to be out forever," Father said, patting me. "It's all over, Mikey. It's all over."

I raised myself only to witness the most horrendous spectacle ever possible in the human imagination. A mass of green slime had covered the entire floor of the auditorium.

Everyone had vomited upon everyone else's lap, smearing the green stuff all over on one another in an effort to hold onto something for help. The entire crowd was asleep, obviously recovering from spewing the toxic green slime out of their bodies. The massive sound from their snoring and twitching in the chairs was something I would never forget.

"This is terrible, this is terrible," I heard the familiar voice of Mr. Yalta, who was surveying the scene. "I have been in two wars but I have never seen anything like this in my whole life."

Then he told me what happened.

After I had bolted out the door with the picture frame under my arm, Miss Casey in no time put two and two together. She correctly guessed that I had figured out that if the sign, "LIBERTY AND JUSTICE FOR ALL," had rid my father of all his Green Palm poison, it should also work on all the others. She immediately contacted Mr. Yalta who might have more of those signs. It so happened that he had several more copies of the sign that he had made. He collected them in a hurry and rushed over to our house. By then, Father had regained enough strength to go with them. Together, they arrived at the auditorium in the nick of time.

"Mikey, you are a hero, now," teased Miss Casey.

The reader too can call me a brave hero. Some townspeople still do call me a hero. But the idea that made me a hero emerged when I was happily splashing water in the bathtub, wishing for some bathtoys.

"You must have had a wild dream, Mikey," Mr. Yalta said. "You were twitching and shaking a quite a bit."

Yes, it was a wild dream—and a nightmare.

It would be many more days before the town of Laurinville recovered from its own nightmare with the Green Palmers. But Laurinville's worst was over. Gradually, everything in our town went back to the way it had been, before the first Green Palm was seen. Everyone returned to the old ways as if nothing had ever happened. To them, perhaps nothing had happened. It was as if the whole town had lost its sanity for some strange reason and recovered just in time to remember nothing of what had happened.

Now Laurinville is as it has always been, with the exception of the 100 days. People no longer lock their doors, nor do they have bars on their windows. Nor does Miss Casey, now Mrs. Brown, still the town's best auto-mechanic, have to contend with "customer-kings." Mr. Dixon quietly removed all the bright colors and posters, and the hidden camera, and no longer puts a "SALE" stamp next to a raised price. Mr. McNamee's bank has gone back to its old ways, without the handsome young vice president for public relations. So has the *Observer,* having dropped the "Crime Report" column because there is nothing to report. Naturally, Mr. Rogers is once again our police chief, his own deputy, dispatcher, ambulance driver, and receptionist. Even Spotty, Mr. Shepeck's guard dog, forgot how to growl and died peacefully amid a great outpouring of sorrows from his neighborhood children. And, of course, the dreaded, brain-sucking tele-mind never came to Laurinville.

My school, where I am now one of the new teachers—oh, what a great place to learn and to love—is clean and friendly once again, the flower gardens having regained their former place as the object of townspeople's voluntary affection. Mrs. Lucy Wilson still teaches, her wonderful and stern self again, and feels strong enough to threaten to teach *my* children when I get married and have my own.

In short, everything is as it has always been. A traveler leaving Laurinville before the Green Palmers and returning after their 100 days would not notice any difference at all.

Well, actually, not everything.

John Sabella never returned home. For years after the Green Palmer incident there were reports of someone, usually from Atkinson, having seen him. But none of those reports led to anything concrete. One rumor had it that he had become a sailor on a merchant ship, vowing never to return home.

The real tragedy, however, turned out to be Mr. Sabella. He still jogs up and down Main Street in his familiar jogging suit. If you jogged alongside him for a while, you would hear him mutter to himself something like "million-dollar athletes," "major league player," "big time contract." Nowadays, no one in Laurinville really understands what he is muttering about, but townspeople say in sympathy that he "has lost his mind."

Personally, I carried the memories of the Green Palmers much longer. My sore limbs and lips reminded me of them for a long time. My encounter with the dreaded tele-mind left a lasting impact on my life and thought. In the next few years or so, I struggled with the world that I had seen through the tele-mind set. It was a world at once wonderful and horrid, fascinating and dreadful, living and dying, and great and terrible. What had been revealed to me through the tele-mind on that fateful day often made me shudder at the frailties of life and morality.

Although everything seemed to have returned to normal in Laurinville, there have been subtle changes. I see hidden fears lurking here and there in the minds and hearts of townspeople, as if the Green Palmers did not really leave them. As for me, the Green Palmers took away my childhood innocence. I could not easily forget the evil they had brought to Laurinville and to our vulnerable hearts. Nor could I easily forget the frightening deterioration of gentle humanity into savagery, at such uncontrollable speed and with such overwhelming force, sending reasonable people into a state of crippling suspicion and doubts about their neighbors.

Not surprisingly, Laurinville has become quite isolated now from what we call the "outside world" so full of evil and fearfulness. We hear that the "town of Laurinville," on its part, has become something of an amusing anachronism to the outside world, a subject of mild curiosity and amusement to other Americans. One report even described us as "a town time forgot." We hear they have coined a new phrase, "doing a Laurinville," to describe anyone who withdraws from the rest of society. In fact, when the president of the United Stated retreated to Camp David for a week, reporters referred to it as "the President still doing his Laurinville." We also hear that great changes have been taking place in the rest of America and the world. But unconcerned, we have slowly retreated into our own safe haven—ourselves—the former state of ourselves—where everything is once again predictable and everyone known and true.

Not too long after the unforgettable day, Mr. Yalta came to our house with a new liberty-and-justice sign to replace the broken one. The new one was much more beautifully crafted than the old one. He hung it up on my bedroom wall as if it would stay there for a hundred years.

"Now, it won't ever fall off again," he said, nailing the frame securely to the wall, "And we don't have the Green Palmers to use it on any more. Not now anyway."

The Green Palmers, Mr. Yalta marvelled, had vanished into thin air in the chaos of the night. They were never again seen in Laurinville.

"They won't come back as long as we live by our new town motto, 'Liberty and Justice for All,'" the watch repairman from

Russia said, yet still slightly worried. I asked him where he thought they had disappeared.

He became thoughtful.

"Well, where they came from, I guess," Mr. Yalta said.

"Where do you think they came from?"

One of the kindest and sweetest human beings I have ever known smiled one of his kind and sweet smiles.

Then he pointed to his heart.

"From here, from within ourselves," he said. "They came, Mikey, from within ourselves."

End of *The Green Palmers*

Comments from Readers

"The book [is] fascinating and disturbing...."
Susan McComb
Ten Speed Press

"A fantastic story! I went from being in suspense in the beginning to being mad at the stupid people [and] to being scared...And just when I thought I knew how it was going to end, it completely threw me off."
Blakely Austin

"It reads a lot like the novels of Stephen King and David Koonce. It uses the self-doubt inside a person on the...evil in oneself to bring out the terror in the reader. The [book] takes the everyday normal things around us and weaves it into something to be afraid of. It is an art form itself to turn [the everyday] into a horror story. A REAL ALL-NIGHT PAGE-TURNER!!"
Michael Duprey

"A very fast-paced story, it does not allow the reader to pause and reflect until the tale is told. The reader is too engrossed in the progress of the story to consider its implications while reading it."
Joseph Fortune

"*THE GREEN PALMERS* examines the progress of America's social degeneration through the eyes of a child, [forcing] us to question ourselves and our society. It provokes thought without ramming the problems afflicting America down the reader's throat. It forces us to look into our hearts and realize that we are all Green Palmers."

Dempsey Green

"[While the book] lives in the heart as a direct story, a story of Small Town, USA, with youth as its dragon slayer, a story for its own sake and yet, although the author never intrudes or points a moral, it also takes on meaning from what we know of affairs of history. To read it is an experience out of the ordinary, as it goes into the region where the heart and the head join together to recognize our values."

Jacob Isbell

"The work is written in a clear and connected narrative. A story line could be followed by a young reader as he explores the changes that occur in an adult world and learn to comprehend through the eyes and questions posed by a 12-year old paper boy roaming the neighborhood.

Simplicity in vocabulary and brevity in sentence structure does not minimize the complexity of the subject. A sophisticated reader will also appreciate the irony and satire in the characters developed."

Steve Kendall

"[As] an allegorical novel, it can be read and appreciated on many different levels. Both children and adults will find the novel interesting and enlightening. Children should like it for its humor and graphic details, such as vomiting up vile green slime. The plot is simple enough for children to follow....Adults should especially enjoy the novel because it is easier for adults to see through the surface and glean the real meaning of the story. [The book] makes it enjoyable for readers of all ages. MAY WE ALL BE SAFE FROM THE GREEN PALMERS."

George Wachter

Printed in the United States
70413LV00002BA/421-447